The Suicide Chronicles

The Suicide Chronicles

By Jabi E. Shriki, MD

The Suicide Chronicles
By Jabi E. Shriki
New Age World Publishing
ISBN: 1-930916-55-8
Copyright © 2003 by Jabi E. Shriki
Cover art by Bradlee Cooper and Jabi E. Shriki

Dedication

This book is dedicated to all the people who offered me help and encouragement during its creation, including Bob Jerdee and Jennifer Chape, Ernie Gonzales, Sacheen Bell and Patricia Arriaga, Jennie Huang, Bradlee Cooper and Sunshine Simeone, Carl Janssen, and Dinah Soriano, and to Roger Pearce for teaching me how to write. It is also dedicated to Marcus Barccani, Ph.D. for his enthusiastic support throughout its publication.

Chapter I

When I was a kid, we expected the end to come abruptly in the form of a catastrophic event that we could prepare for and say, "This is it. This is the end." A nuclear war, a comet from outer space, a global, environmental disaster—the end of humanity would be something we could see coming that would mark for us the day of doom. No one was really prepared when changes happened subtly. Perhaps it was our arrogance as a race that made us expect the end of humanity would come only with the end of the world. Even as humanity decayed, the world endured. It changed slightly and slowly wedged us out of our comfortable niche; but for the most part, outside of the human species, life went on and even flourished.

The progression of events that chiseled away the civilization we had constructed was slow enough that no one suspected that the end had come until it was too late. Gradually, the sky slowly changed its color from the blue skies that some of us remembered from our youth to the gray haze that crept up along the horizon. At the same time, weather patterns changed; less rain, too much rain, rain in the wrong places at the wrong times—changes so subtle that, had they been a little slower, we might have been able to adapt. Instead, we ignored the changes, while the agricultural sector began losing crops and entire supplies of food. In the early turn of the century, the decimation of corn production caused a food shortage in South America. A few years later, wheat crops in India and Bangladesh failed resulting in a tremendous shortage of bread and grains in those countries. One-by-one other significant crops around the world began to fail, and the shortage of food became more and more pronounced.

Changing weather patterns slowly destabilized populations in other ways. Before long, tens of thousands of lives were being lost every year to flooding, drought, and natural disasters. In the Middle East, where water was always scarce, flooding in some parts contaminated the few existing clean water reservoirs. The scarce water began to be hoarded by some countries from the vanishing rivers. Other countries, often downstream, lost their water supply altogether. It didn't take long for the more water-poor countries to resort to weapons of mass destruction to cajole rival nations, and eventually decimate much of the population. Further east, in India and Pakistan, the onset of flooding uprooted thousands of families and resulted in worsening political instability and wars over clean water supplies. The expanding rich-poor gap in much of Asia caused upheavals to turn into revolutions, and border disputes to turn into wars.

I suppose another part of the problem is that the onslaught of ecological change wasn't really felt by the more industrialized nations. For the most part, the countries that were hit hardest by the climate changes were Third World, under-industrialized countries. For some reason, the evolving natural disasters seemed to only directly hit those countries that, ironically, were weren't as responsible for breaking nature's back. Since the effects took longer to impact the First World nations, action around the planet was slow and ineffectual.

While humanity wasted time and ignored the changing global climate, the insects of the world found these changes more and more favorable. North America was overwhelmed by locusts in the early turn of the century; later, Europe became overrun with beetles and roaches. A few species, which were once mild nuisances, became more aggressive, like the killer bees in the Southwest of America, and the thorned ants, which descended upon village after village in Central America. Everywhere else, there were markers that the insects were now asserting their rightful claim over the globe. Ants in kitchens and bathrooms became more ubiquitous. It became even impossible to keep some of the more tenacious species away from the food supply, both on the individual and industrial levels.

And the rising tide of insects brought new and more vicious diseases to the rest of the human population. Viral encephalitis, an infection of the brain transmitted by insects, became a common source of death. Malaria and other tropical diseases became more commonplace in much of the coastal United States, Mexico, and Canada. New diseases were appearing faster and outpacing the ability of the medical field to devise treatments.

But by the time the First World realized that humanity was descending into a crisis, it was too late for any intervention to be effective. The human response was to muster up technology to reclaim our hold on the environment. Massive tracts of land were sprayed with pesticides and more broad-spectrum toxins. As we realized we were descending into a crisis, we became more audacious, implementing new tactics with less regard for the well being of even our own species. Some chemicals, which proved to be effective against insects were used before studies on their safety could even be completed---steps that a once cautious and pragmatic species now deemed necessary to regain our foothold on the globe we had for so long taken for granted. The race to save humanity, in part, became a race between the evolutionary adaptability of the insect kingdom, and the technological resourcefulness of humans. As history unfolded, our technology proved somewhat effective against the would-be rulers of the Earth, but the real successes of our science would require more profound sacrifices on our part.

In the middle of the 21st century, a bold leader of the European Union of Nations, Uri Reltichev, under desperate circumstances and pressures from a near-starving population, announced a plan to construct a city free of insects in one of the more temperate regions of the Ukraine. The plan called for construction of the city over a demolished and deforested area, which was thoroughly and rigorously sprayed with the latest insecticides once it was leveled. Then, in the place of uncontrolled nature, a city would be developed surrounded by walls of physical and chemical barriers to insects. The prototypical city, New Khotovsk, was erected near the turn of the 22nd century. On its perimeter there were placed pumps, which bellowed extensive insecticides and insect repellents into the air. Just within these, there was a perimeter of motors and air circulators to generate favorable air currents and keep the chemicals outside of the city so that more effective and more toxic substances could be used. Giant air purifiers in rows and fields of ionizing radiation stood forming the next border. The radiation served the purpose of deactivating any stray particles of insecticide. Finally, the innermost boundary was a physical barrier with giant electrified walls. Within the confines of this city of the future, there would be some technologically advanced agriculture, enough to make this city or one like it, be self-sufficient some day. The first plans drawn up were fairly crude; and, after billions of dollars and man-hours of construction, its residents abandoned New Khotovsk within a matter of months. While New Khotovsk was deemed a failure, this new city did establish the idea for several other national undertakings. The idea was to construct a Maginot Line behind which humanity could entrench itself, if not flourish. Several other nations and aggregates of nations followed suit, improving the design of the perimeter as well as the self-sufficiency of the microcosm of human society within each city. Each project was more elaborate and insect-free than its predecessor.

As the new cities grew larger and more comfortable, they eventually seemed utopian to those living outside them. The rest of society, in the meantime, had to adapt to living in a world more overrun with insects where food was becoming increasingly scarce. By the end of the twenty-first century, people in most regions couldn't even sleep through the night without waking up once or twice to shake off the row of ants marching up their bed sheets. At first, residents of the new cities were selected from among the few who volunteered, but as humanity realized we were peering down the barrel of extinction, volunteers became more and more abundant, and the selection criteria adopted by governments for residents became more exclusive. I imagine the feeling was like being on one of the lifeboats of the sinking Titanic watching humans all around you dying while trying to climb into the already over-filled boats. In this case, people succumbed to the lack of food, the unfavorable climate change, and the ever-encroaching march of insects. The ultimate future for humanity seemed unavoidable, and people clung to any chance for survival. At the beginning, no one thought these new civilizations to be the only refuge for humanity; at most these fortresses would merely be a way that humanity could temporarily retreat and regroup so that someday, when the dangers subsided, humans would go back to populating the entire globe. Somehow the survivors of the new cities lost sight of that hope.

Another unexpected attitude was the disregard that developed for the rest of the human world. I suppose as people saw these cities of the future as the only hope, residents of the old cities began to resent their circumstances. Many of the more important individuals and would-be community leaders of the old cities, who could have helped the rest of humanity, opted to instead find residence in a new city. Some people felt like these new civilizations were nothing more than zoos for humans, but this wasn't the general attitude. The rest of the population lost faith in efforts to keep the rest of the world habitable. Not as much effort was put into making agriculture more efficient, or improving the air. Each individual's goal was to somehow earn a position in the new human order, rather than to improve the old way of life. The rest of the world, consequently, began to deteriorate. Industry, agriculture, and infrastructure slowly decayed, as technology was hoarded in the new cities.

The next step in this chronology was even uglier. Initially, the residents of a city were, generally, those people who were deemed more useful to their respective communities, and selection criteria were based on this utilitarian perspective. As time passed though, a glaring inequity developed, as the members of the cities that were established proved also to be the more affluent members of society. Although this was at first justified by the argument that these were the scientists and engineers who could be of the greatest use to the rest of humanity, a wave of sentiment passed across the world that there was a class-based and racial motivation for the selection of "survivors."

Shortly after the 23rd century, a cooperative new city project between Canada and the United States, Pacifica, was engulfed in a huge uprising. The city was overrun and destroyed by rioters. The uprising left the new city in ruins, and several tens of thousands of residents and outsiders died from the ensuing violence and the spread of toxic fumes that made up the barriers of Pacifica. After that, a wave of panic hit other cities, which bolstered their defenses. Several other riots occurred, but rioters were less successful penetrating the walls of other cities. Perhaps part of the reason for this was that people elsewhere saw how much everyone suffered as a result of what happened in uprising at Pacifica. Another, reason, though, may have been the steps to intensify the defensive and insecticidal walls around cities. It was hard enough for rioters to get through the walls of insecticides at Pacifica, but as subsequent cities upgraded their Maginot Lines, the defenses against intruders were designed not only to fend off insect invaders, but also to keep out other humans. Contempt within the new cities for the remainder of the human population grew.

On the other hand, within these lines, humanity did flourish, even as the rest of the world languished. A few of the residents of the most advanced cities were working to make the entire globe more habitable. But in the short-run, only the residents of new cities were able to experience the benefits of newer technology. For example, as science advanced, ways were discovered to cure diseases and extend the lifespan of humans. Remarkable technological developments even uncovered ways to retard the aging process.

Medical advances had to be coupled with efforts to control the population. As people lived longer, cities faced issues of balancing an expanding population with finite resources. Therefore, reproduction within the new cities was highly regulated. In most of the new cities, any one who opted to have life-extending and anti-aging treatment had to accept sterilization so the new cities could avoid the eventuality of overpopulation.

That's the choice I made, it seemed natural to want to live longer rather than have children. My wife Belinda, felt the same, I guess we thought that we could postpone the decision to have children until later on, when the world got better, and the danger to humanity had passed.

I guess you'd say I was one of the lucky ones in the changing world order. As a scientist, I was selected at a young age, in my twenties, to live in one of the new cities that was being established on the east coast of North America, called Chesapeake City. It was one of the larger and more modern cities of our time. By that time, countries of North and Central America were working jointly to build the new cities. My experience as a scientist wasn't the only factor that earned me residency; I also had an uncle who had sat on a planning commission for another one of the new cities, who pulled at least a few strings to get me a residence.

Belinda met me while I was still planning to leave the rest of the world. I had just finished working on my doctoral thesis in agricultural engineering. We met in a grocery market, which was becoming more and more a place for the affluent as food everywhere became more scarce. You could almost judge a person's wealth by their groceries. Belinda was young and beautiful with smooth round eyes, and soft brown hair. As soon as it was announced that I was to be transferred, we were married so that she could stay with me in Chesapeake City.

When I left the outside world, the downward slide of humanity was already apparent. The older cities were starting to decay; urban crime was on the rise; and the inner-city problems were encroaching on the rest of society as the borders of crime-infested neighborhoods grew in size and the impoverished grew in number.

Belinda was not from as important a family as I was, and she would have been a casualty of crime and urban depression were it not for her association with me.

As soon as I was in Chesapeake City, I began working as an agricultural engineer. Initially, my duties included overseeing the city's crops with several other scientists and, hopefully, also contributing to the research and development of better strains of plants. The research was focused on building better, more efficient crops that produced more fruit more often, and required fewer natural resources to thrive.

For the first few years, our lives in Chesapeake City was every bit the utopian ideal that I had expected. Our living quarters were very comfortable, the city was free of crime, all the residents were friendly, and clean air and food were abundant.

As a scientist I have invested much of my life in advancing technology and advocating the importance of research and development, but I have to admit that while trying to solve one problem, science often creates another. Belinda used to want nothing more than to have a family, as we grew older, though, she became more comfortable with sacrificing the option of parenthood to preserve her youth. Like almost every other resident, we opted to be temporarily sterilized to attain anti-aging treatment regimens.

The therapy consisted of enhancing our bodies' own biological DNA repair mechanisms to complement our cells' means of repairing damage. Special, genetically altered enzymes like telomerases were added to some of our cell lines to keep our cells in reproduction. Some of the cells of our cutaneous and subcutaneous tissues underwent *ex vivo* genetic reprogramming to continuously rebuild our outer layers of skin and preserve a youthful appearance. It must sound like an elaborate and complicated procedure, but science found ways to make the therapy less invasive. Eventually, the frequency of treatments could be reduced to once a month, and later, to once every few months. In the end, death was still unavoidable, but life and the proportion of life spent in one's youth, were much longer.

Most other residents chose the same therapy—almost everyone, in fact, did. And the population within each city aged without growing older. Of course, a few problems with this therapy arose with certain people. Some cell lines could not be well preserved in certain people, especially neurons, and in these people, senility was inevitable, or so the medical community told us. There were rare individuals whose mental status deteriorated over time. The process was more pronounced in some than in others, and this problem seemed to affect only a minority of people. Sometimes, you would see someone who looked like they were in their thirties or forties, but acted sedated and senile. I was lucky that Belinda hadn't shown much of a change as we aged.

The new cities were left with a small, aging population of less productive individuals, some growing more docile and ineffective. For some, the only humane option was to discontinue therapy and let them live out the rest of their lives in less shame. Others were more loathsome to give up their therapy. In rare cases, the city's authorities had to slowly marginalize individuals who had become less able to perform their jobs. To replace this slow attrition process, some couples were allowed to have children. Overtime, the next generation could be trained to perform jobs to replace previous generations.

When children reached school age, the education process wasn't as open ended as higher education in the outside world, though. Instead, the process was highly vocationalized. Each child was, from his or her youth, trained to work in a specific position, usually in a specific vacancy left from a particular individual.

Belinda and I had been living in the city for fifteen years, and we had each settled into our own routines, which became gradually more comfortable as the days progressed. I would go to work in the mornings and come home in the afternoons or evenings each day. Belinda was either making dinner or socializing with some of the other wives in the area until I arrived. That's how she spent her days. I didn't find as much time for a social life as she did. My work was fairly demanding. As I said, I was a scientist in the agricultural industry of Chesapeake City; working to design newer, more robust plants that could function as a food source in an environment of limited natural and geographical resources. My work involved so many interactions with my colleagues, that, when I did have spare time, I chose to spend it alone. Mostly I would walk alone on the streets of Chesapeake City in the evenings.

The city wasn't dark at night, and the streetlights drowned out the stars. Except for the sky, which was a darker hue of blue at night, you really could scarcely tell that it was night at all. Of course, for reasons of efficiency, all the lights in the street were shut off at a certain time of night, after which, all the residents were required to be in their homes. This law was enforced by a small, private police force, but almost everyone in the city complied willingly.

I almost always made it home before the city's lights were turned off every night, except for one night, when for some reason, I had walked a little further than usual. For no particular reason, on that night, it took me a little while longer to make it home, and the city lights were shut off before I could arrive back at my living quarters. While I was on my way home, I heard a man yelling; his voice was gruff with anger, so I followed the sound. I wasn't sure if I thought he might have been in trouble or if I was acting in anticipation of what happened next. I peered down a darkened alley where I thought the noise was coming from. As I did, I heard a woman's whimper.

"Is everything alright?" I called out.

"No it isn't," was the reply I heard.

As my eyes were still adjusting to the darkness, I vaguely saw the outline of a man moving towards me. I swung out my right arm; maybe to defend myself, maybe just to see what was in front of me. I felt my fist connecting with his shoulder, and he fell backwards for a moment. He lunged at me again, but I dodged his move forward and swung again. This time, I hit his face with more resolution in my swing. As he backed away, I pushed him against the wall. I heard the sound as the back of his head knocking against the wall behind him.

He was a good deal smaller than I was, and the fight would have been pretty unmatched had it continued; he was angry enough that he seemed willing to fight as long as he was able. This changed when the police force showed up. As I noticed their lights outlining our shadows against the wall, he began to cry for help. I let go of him, but he fell to the ground as though I had badly beaten him.

As the lights from the police vehicle filled up the alley, I looked at the other figure, a woman with bruises covering her eyes and face. Rather than question us on the spot, the police subdued and arrested us quickly and without saying anything. They then transported all three of us to a nearby department. I was sitting in the middle, in the back seat of the police car, and sharing a very uncomfortable silence. We were all immediately thrown into a detention cell.

The prison system in the outside world had long since deteriorated, but the local jails of the new cities were still relatively well maintained. In the new cities, temporary detention cells were privately maintained by commercial companies, which were contracted by each city's governance. This jail cell had three beds along the walls of the room. Each had a cage around the bed that gave your body little room to move. Law enforcement was privatized and poorly regulated, and the authority of the law enforcers gradually expanded to include judicial powers in sentencing. The rest of society stopped caring what happened when people broke the law, especially in the new cities. Crime was a messy problem that was better left in the hands of an efficiently run, private police force that could carry out punishment more swiftly than the cumbersome judicial system of the outside world. Besides, crime was supposed to be something that happened outside of the walls of the new cities, a remnant of a human civilization that the residents of new cities were trying to forget existed.

The three of us spent several hours in silence, as the police officers instructed us to say nothing. We were awakened early in the morning at about two a.m., wearing the same clothing we had on the night before, and escorted to a small hearing before a police Captain under heavily armed guards. We were taking directly from our cell into the room before this captain. I asked immediately about my wife, and if I could contact her, but before I could finish he interrupted me and said, "She knows where you are."

The captain was a chubby man with a small chin out of proportion to his long face, which seemed to be constantly contorted in a grave grimace.

"I'll be brief with you," he started. "Living in this city is a privilege. A privilege extended to very, very few people. Maybe you've forgotten what the outside world is like. I'll tell you, and I'll tell you more. Civilization has very few chances, and Chesapeake City is one of them. So somebody had better give me a damn good reason why I should let people inside this civilization fight like monkeys—like monkeys—in the streets." He was quiet for most of his speech, but he would burst into shouting to emphasize key points, for example, the word "monkeys." Although he was trying to sound angered, his speech ended up sounding practiced and oratorical. I found it hard to take his authoritative demeanor seriously as he paced back and forth in front of us.

As I sized-up the situation I was in, I realized certain things didn't portend a favorable outcome me. For example, I was the least beaten-up person in the room. Also, when the police found us, I was doing most of the fighting and probably looked like the aggressor. Fortunately for me, the officer seemed unconcerned with any of these details. Nor did he care about finding out what exactly happened the previous night. Instead, he seemed to want to make his point and then expediently dismiss the situation, and he had little concern with the details of what exactly happened. Looking back, it seemed like we weren't in his office for more than a few minutes.

Although he directed most of his shouting at me, the officer gave the same punishment to the three of us. He stated, that he was placing all of us on probation, which is may only sound like a slap on the wrist, but in the new cities, probation was a rather serious measure. First, it carries a social stigma that is difficult to erase, and a stigma that is more far-reaching than you might expect. Second, probation mars your record as a resident, and any further violations of city rules could result in deportation from the city.

I was able to return to Belinda that night and to go to work the next day, even though I hadn't gotten much sleep. When I came home, Belinda was asleep, but she woke up when I got into bed. I started to tell her what happened.

"I know what happened", she said. "They called and told me." I could tell from the tone of her voice that she didn't intend to express sympathy.

"Listen, Belinda," I said trying to defend myself. "I was just out walking a little late when I heard this couple fighting in the alley. I was on my way home, and the man in the couple attacked me."

"You shouldn't have been out that late, anyway. You shouldn't go walking late at night like that. You're asking for trouble when you do that", she said.

I realized she had just woken up, and I probably wasn't going to be able to change her mind about what happened.

"I know," I said. "I'm sorry if I worried you." She had been lying in the same position, facing away from me, for most of the conversation. "I'll let you go back to sleep. We can talk more tomorrow."

Belinda didn't say anything else, and I went to sleep. We ended up not bringing up the subject the next day. I didn't feel like defending myself further. But Belinda did make sure I took fewer and shorter evening walks.

I was a little tired the next day, but after this event, both of our lives fell back into our comfortable routines for many more months. Work seemed to still go okay, and Belinda and I were still very much enjoying the material comfort we had in Chesapeake City.

Chapter II

While for many years, life in Chesapeake City was every bit the utopian ideal I had hoped it would be, things slowly began to change, and most of the changes happened within a few months of my being put on probation. First of all, I noticed people didn't treat me the same way after my probation, although no one ever really asked me about what happened. To my knowledge, no one around me except Belinda found out about my arrest. At the same time, it seemed like my career was beginning to suffer, and I noticed I wasn't performing as well at work. At least I was cognizant of these changes as they were happening, though. Other times, I was oblivious even as my very life was falling apart around me. For example, my relationship with Belinda was also deteriorating, but by the time I realized things were going badly with her, she had long since been seeing someone else.

My health began to deteriorate over time, as well. It was rare to be sick for any length of time in Chesapeake City; residents had access to some of the most advanced medical treatments in the world. But I started feeling ill more often. From time to time, I would have little aches and pains that wouldn't go away as quickly as they used to, and I would catch a cold or get an annoying cough more often, even while everyone around me seemed fine.

None-the-less, I felt that things weren't going too badly, at least for a couple of years. I wasn't working any less hard than anyone else, and I wasn't living in the outside world, so I was satisfied with my life. On the other hand, I was beginning to feel more marginalized at the plant where I worked. When I first joined the center, the other researchers welcomed me in; but after a few months, they seemed less and less enthusiastic about associating with me. My conversations with the other workers there became more forced. Once in a while, when I ate lunch with someone else, they would do most of the talking asking me a lot of questions in an attempt to make small talk or find common ground. I found myself eating lunch more and more often alone. And every once in a while I would catch people rolling their eyes or shaking their heads after something I said—not directly at me, more out of the corner of my eye, but I still noticed.

As my interactions with others felt less comfortable, I began to associate with others less often. Despite the subtle problems that I had, I didn't give too much thought to how well I was fitting in. At the time it didn't seem that important.

While I never had problems socializing before, I was also never especially good at it; nor was I good at being the type of person who gets ahead because everyone likes him or her. That always made me work harder for good grades in school, and eventually, research grants, and promotions in my career. I knew that if I were going to get ahead in life, it wouldn't be because other people liked me; it would be because I had earned my recognition.

More than my disconcertment with my lack of a social life, I was now becoming more disturbed by the changes that I saw going on in myself. Little intellectual tasks that were once easier for me were starting to become more difficult. In the research plant, I didn't seem to be doing as well at work. Once, another researcher and I were examining gaseous mixtures in order to find an atmospheric mixture that would best facilitate growth of certain plants. During one experiment, we were spraying certain chemicals into the gases to determine how well we could grow edible fungi in a hostile environment. Apparently, I had forgotten to circulate the atmosphere and administer certain vital nutrients to the fungi we were growing. The next day, none of the fungi were still viable. When the other researcher saw how damaged the crop was, he became irate and yelled about how I was wasting resources—wasting the potential food supply we were trying to create.

My coworker was upset and stormed off. Not too much later that day, I was called into the office of the manager of the research center. My supervisor, Mark Alder, was a tall man with sunken eyes and low brows. He was always pleasant and friendly, but was also so tactful in his approach to people; and when someone is that meticulously trying to be genuine, it's hard to tell if they're truly being friendly, or if they're just very good at covering up apathy or malevolence. I often wondered if Adler was sincerely happy to interact with me, or if he was just skillful at acting. Adler was a scientist like me, but he was also something of a politician, and he gained his position of power in a very different way than the way I gained mine. Maybe I wasn't entirely justified, but I imagined that Adler was the type of person who did get ahead because everyone liked him.

He started off with the normal salutations, offering me a drink, and making sure I was comfortable. "I wanted to talk about your relationships with the other employees," he said.

I said nothing for a moment—hopeful that he wouldn't bring up the experiment I had ruined.

"How do you think you've been getting along with others?"

"I think I've adjusted pretty well, I consider most everyone here to be a close friend." It was a lie, but I thought that this was probably what Adler wanted to hear.

"Well, that's kind of what I wanted to talk to you about," Adler said. Some of the other people working here don't know how receptive you've been with them."

"I'm not sure who that would be. Quite a few people have confided in me at one time or another. People consider me their friend." My defense was flimsy and transparent.

"All right that's good... good... Still some people have the sentiment that you have been a little difficult to work with at times." Adler was displaying his artful manner of dealing with people. I could see how hard he was working, while bringing up this sensitive subject with me.

"Well," I said. "I've been trying not to lose sight of why we're all here." I was grasping to try to defend myself. "This isn't a collective effort to get better acquainted with each other. We're trying to find a way to prolong our existence as a species. I can see how sometimes, I might focus on the larger goal of our work here."

"That's actually part of the problem. You've been here quite a long time and you haven't really produced anything ... substantial enough in quite a while." I was somewhat offended, but I didn't have much of a defense for that accusation.

"I kind of was slow to adjust to all this—"

"That's true, and that's what I told people too, including some of your coworkers, including some of my supervisors who have asked how you've been adjusting in Chesapeake City. And I've stuck my neck out for you, believe it or not, quite a few times, but I just can't keep making excuses." At times during the conversation, I was almost sympathetic to Adler. He was so adept at convincing me that he really did have my best interests at heart.

"If there's anything you would suggest I do..."

"Well, sort of," he said. "Look. I want you to know that this isn't anything personal. It's nothing I hold against you. But even the higher-ups, some of my supervisors, have noticed that you're not producing much, and to be honest, the availability of space in the city is limited. Everyone here should feel privileged that they have a life here, and should work hard to help out the rest of the city. You're here now and no one's going to force you out, but we would hope that everyone here would try their hardest to contribute both at work and in society. It's hard enough to get along, all of us in the confines of what is really a small geographical area."

"I understand." I didn't really, I had been working hard and doing everything that was asked of me. In the past, I was always somewhat unnerved that Adler could say almost anything to anyone and yet be so unemotional, and I felt this even more as I sat in Adler's office. There was never even so much as a bead of perspiration on his forehead during this conversation, and his finely combed and gelled hair was never the least bit disheveled.

As I rode the transport home from work that day, I wondered what Adler was talking about. Who had come forward to complain about me? So many people had showed vague signs of dislike for me, but they were all so minor, I never thought to take any of them seriously.

At the same time, my home life wasn't going much better. I suppose by then my relationship with Belinda had already started deteriorating, although I didn't know it at the time. Later, looking back, I could see some of the signs that she wasn't happy with our relationship. When I knew her in the outside world, she had always talked about having children—something that I thought would be a good idea someday. Once we lived in Chesapeake City, though, she didn't show any interest in applying to become pregnant. I realized it would have been a sacrifice, but I almost wished she would be more regretful about giving up on parenthood. Before we lived in Chesapeake City, she was anxious to go out and spend time with me. Now, she was becoming less interested in socializing by my side. I remembered once the way that her smile gave her eyes an almond shape, but gradually, I began to see, out of the corner of my eye, the subtle looks of disdain that I was so familiar with at work. I grew distant from her much more quickly than I did from the scientists in my research plant. Sometimes, I felt resentful that Belinda was less warm to me once we moved into the city. I even felt that perhaps she had used me to get a ticket to a better life than what she would have had otherwise.

Outside of her relationship with me, Belinda was getting along quite well in Chesapeake City. She often had plans to socialize and I had thought that she must have made quite a few friends. Over the next years, she socialized more and more apart from me. One night, she didn't come home. When I asked her where she had been she became defensive.

"Why didn't you call me or try to contact me?" she said.

I told her I was sure she was safe wherever she was. There aren't any real threats when you live in one of the new cities.

"Weren't you the least bit worried about me?"

"Well, I didn't think there was any reason." I was very concerned about my relationship with Belinda, but foolishly, I thought that seeming upset or angry that she had been out would have further soured our relationship.

After I realized she was upset by my apparent apathy, I did try asking her where she had gone, but she said she was upset with me and didn't want to discuss it. Our relationship continued to deteriorate. The few times we spent together were spent in silence. I didn't suspect how bad things had gotten, until she packed her things and left. I found out later that there were other reasons she had been growing so distant. I suspected that she must have had another relationship. After all, she couldn't just move out on her own in Chesapeake City; residence was strictly regulated and restricted, and I knew she wouldn't leave Chesapeake City just to get away from me, no matter how bad our relationship had become. Still, I had no idea who her new relationship could have been with.

The next few days were taxing, but strangely, after Belinda moved out, I felt a little bit relieved. At least now I had a living unit to myself. That, I thought, might make it easier to unwind and relax, and maybe I'd be more productive at work. It didn't help much, though, according to my coworkers. By then, even I was beginning to understand that there was something more seriously wrong with the way I was thinking. My power of denial protected me from the truth for a surprisingly long time, but soon, my problems were becoming too apparent to ignore.

One afternoon, while I was riding home from work on a transport, I noticed a familiar face. The man standing just a few feet away from me seemed vaguely familiar. As I focused on him and searched my memory, I realized he was the same small man that I had fought with in the dark alley so many months ago. It had been a long time, but that night made such an impression on me, that I could still remember his face. At some point, he looked back at me, too. I noticed the glazed expression in his eyes. This was not the energetic, angered little man that I had beaten up. I hoped he wouldn't remember me, and I don't think he did. He looked at me for a while, probably because I had been looking at him, and then looked away, staring off into space, possibly hoping that I didn't remember him either.

About a month later, I apparently ruined another experiment and wasted a great deal of supplies in my neglect. Neglect alone can be a very serious offense in the city. Since the city is based on the notion of maximal efficiency, wastefulness is not tolerated. Adler called me into his office to explain to me that he and some of the other employees were going to file a petition with the city council to have me removed from my job, and in essence, from Chesapeake City.

"I'm sorry, that I have to do this to you."

"That's all right," I said.

"It's nothing personal and I'm not trying to do this to hurt you personally in any way."

"I understand."

I knew that bickering with Adler would achieve nothing. He was far too adept at dealing with people for me to even make him angry or even shake his emotional equanimity. Besides, I didn't have the energy to argue.

Once you're in the city, if you attend work and do what you're told it's very hard to be fired from a job. In the worse cases of poor work, you might be reassigned to a task of more menial labor—some of the more unpleasant tasks that still needed to be done. If an employee continues to be neglectful, or is more extremely unmotivated or incompetent, they can, then, be thrown out of the city. It doesn't really make sense to fire anyone, since the existence of an unemployed population in the city would be wasteful and inefficient. You weren't accepted into the city to be unproductive. But if someone is unproductive enough at his or her primary job, then they may initially be thrown out.

I'm sure this makes Chesapeake City sound very authoritarian. It wasn't. But it was realistically utopian. The city didn't tell you what to do with your life. You did whatever you did on the outside world. Like other cities, Chesapeake City decided whether or not what you did was something that they needed. When the city needed more individuals in a profession, they were recruited from the outside world, although the rest of the world was beginning to provide dwindling resources from the perspective of the new cities.

The city council and mayorship were, as one might imagine, a very concentrated source of political power in the new cities. This system evolved for two reasons. First, in the outside world, there were so many lawyers and would-be politicians that the amount of governmental power had to be divided up into smaller amounts so that power could be shared among more people. When it came to living in a city, though, too few lawyers and politicians could justify the claim that their contribution to a given city would be useful. Second, in the outside world, national, and state authorities checked the authority of a city. Since the new cities became such autonomous microcosms of civilization, the city governments became the sole source of political power.

The worse punishment that the city would ever levy would be exportation. It wasn't worth the time or effort to build a prison system for incarceration of people who weren't productive, and capital punishment was considered to be a tool that was only needed in the outside world. In the early days of the new cities, exportation wasn't considered as much of a horrible punishment. Back then, since the outside world hadn't yet become such a wasteland, people who were exported from a city weren't cast out to their demise. The laws though, for exporting citizens of a city stayed in effect, though, long after the outside world decayed. The de facto provision that protected people was that fewer citizens were expelled from the new cities over time, and the judging criteria of the city council for exporting citizens became much narrower.

As a result, I wasn't too worried the day of my hearing. It had been years since I had heard of a citizen being exported, and I knew of many cases of individuals more deserving of exportation than I, which were looked on favorably by the city council. I had hoped that, at least, I could be relegated to a lower profession; surely, the city could make use of me in some way. Maybe I seemed too confident before the city council, or maybe I was just unlucky, but the cards didn't fall in my favor that day.

I prepared for my hearing as though I was preparing for a day at work. I had made a few notes of the things I wanted to say, but I wasn't prepared for the magnitude of the attack that would be made against me. Almost all of my co-workers spoke on Dr. Adler's behalf to attest to my incompetence. The procession of individuals lasted until relatively late in the afternoon. Since I didn't say much throughout, the process moved along more quickly. I wanted to say more to defend myself, but I didn't want to seem cantankerous, and give the council hearing my case any reason to dislike me.

The hearing took place in a large room paneled with imitation wood, and each speaker's words reverberated against the hard walls. Lights beamed down on top of me from above the council's bench. By the end of the day, I was so exhausted by the entire process, as well as the uncomfortable heat in the room, that I was unable to say much in my defense. I did, though, believe that none of the accidents at work were my fault, and I also asserted that I still had a great deal to offer Chesapeake City.

Although I shouldn't have been surprised when the council rendered their decision, I had the uncanny feeling that, had I been expecting a negative decision, it wouldn't have been rendered. Things weren't working out for me, and it seemed that whenever I prepared for something, the opposite would happen.

I left the tall, gray council building on my way back home and passed Alder receiving a congratulatory hug from Belinda.

Chapter III

The day after my hearing, I received a brief letter from the city indicating that I should be ready to leave by 8:30 the next morning. I was sitting down, and as I read it, and I slumped over in my chair realizing the finality of the city's enjoinder to me. I sat there for a few hours—dazed by the blow that had been struck. This would be among the last few hours of comfort that I would feel for a long time.

Finally, I stood up and walked around my living quarters, trying to pick out what I should take with me when I left. As I looked around my residence, I realized that I couldn't take much with me; much of it, like the furniture and appliances, was the property of Chesapeake City. The rest of my meager possessions couldn't even be helpful in the outside world. I also realized how little attachment I had to the objects in my living quarters. Very little of what I included in my surroundings seemed special to me. I wasn't sure what to choose, but I ended up packing some trinkets and utensils for myself, which I would later find to be extremely useless.

The atmosphere on the perimeter of the city is highly toxic. The thick wall of pesticides is necessary to protect the residents, but I was worried, that I wouldn't be able to make it through. To this end, the government of Chesapeake City gave me protective clothing and a small satchel for my possessions. One item I took was a small knife-like utensil. Most weapons were highly regulated to the necessary police forces within the city, but I thought, that a knife—even though it was a small, cooking knife—might offer me some protection once I reached the outside world.

As the letter advised me, at 8:30 the next morning, a police vehicle with two young-looking officers picked me up from my residency quarters and brought me to the outer wall. They shared the silence with me very awkwardly. One of the officers had a small, patchy goatee; the other had a face covered with acne. I had to imagine that the two of them must have, only recently come to Chesapeake City. I also guessed that escorting exportees out of the city was considered a lowly responsibility, probably relegated to newcomers and rookies on the security force. As the vehicle exited the one of the outer walls, the officers sealed off the air supply to the front of the vehicle and turned on what must have been a number of air filters and oxygen pumps. The car took me through each wall and barrier into a thicker and thicker haze of chemicals.

Before I left the car, I was given a mask and supply of oxygen to traverse the perimeter of the city. But once I was sent on my way, I immediately realized how ill-equipped I was to face the outside atmosphere. As soon as I left the outermost wall of Chesapeake City, the thick hue of chemicals became attached to my skin like a sticky film, and my skin itched and burned underneath. My eyes began to blur and water as I stared out through the chemical cloud. I could breath, but my chest felt tight like a band was being wrapped around my torso. I was pushed on by the turbines, which guided the polluted air away from the city and against my back. They were remarkably strong even at some distance.

I had been walking for several hours when I began to run out of oxygen. By this point, my fingers were sticking together and my skin had taken on a yellow-purple color. Fortunately, the density of the pesticides was beginning to remit. So I pushed on further without the use of a gas mask.

After a couple hours more, out of either exhaustion or delirium, I decided to rest. My clothes, even underneath the protective gear, were badly soiled and discolored, and they felt thick and stiff, saturated with fumes, as I moved each of my limbs. I discarded most of the items of clothing I was wearing, rather than trying to clean them. Instead, I changed into another set of clothing that I had been carrying in my satchel. The air was still thick, but I had moved far enough away, that I thought I would be all right. After what I had just been through, the atmosphere now seemed much cleaner.

At some point afterwards, I guess the toxic fumes began to take their toll on me neurologically. I sat down to take a rest at some point. The last thing I remember was experiencing a vision from my child hood—not so much a daydream, but rather a reverie. I was five years old, sitting with my family under a tree; it was a picnic. My mother was there, but not my father; they divorced when I was very young. There was a string of males in my mother's life after the divorce; I understood only later their relationship to my mother. I don't remember which one it was sitting there underneath the tree with my mother and I. There were so many of them that my recollections melted together my memories of each one. The face I remembered was the face of a man, but it was non-descript, without detail—almost without an identity.

While sitting under the tree, I remembered, at some point we were swarmed by insects. First, two or three came and swooped down onto our picnic food. They were quickly followed by a swarm of others. My mother and the man who was with her reacted with an annoyed anger, not at the insects, but rather at each other. I don't remember why. This must have been at a time that her relationship with one of the men in her life was beginning to fail. Here's where the memories changed. The insects in my reverie turned from the food we had, and began attacking me. They started by biting at my feet, and then gradually began taking bigger and more aggressive bites out of the rest of my arms and legs. Finally, they were surrounding my face. All the while my mother and the man were still arguing and failed to notice what was happening to me. I tried to scream, but I had no voice. I tried to claw them off my skin, but I was paralyzed. I heard the buzzing and chirping sounds they made becoming more and more real in my ears. I was still disoriented of course, thinking that I was still a five-year-old boy at a picnic. In a moment of lucidity, I finally opened my eyes. Though my vision was badly blurred, I could tell that this part of my dream had become real. I realized the sounds of my mother and her companion yelling were the voices of two other people who were now there with me while I regained consciousness; they were yelling instructions at each other as they tried to scrape the insects off my skin and head. Their voices were now becoming distant through the buzzing of insects inside my ear canals.

I must have showed some signs of consciousness, since the two individuals started telling me not to move around so much, but I don't remember anything else. I stopped moving.

It must have been a few weeks later that I woke up. My mind seemed to come back slowly and it became less foggy with time. I have very hazy memories that include waking up covered in sweat and with vomit dripping from my chin. I have other memories of trying to scratch the scabs off my itchy skin. The first lucid memory that I had included both of these. It felt like someone was pulling something out of my throat. I remember the sounds of their voices slowly coming into focus.

"Stop scratching. You'll only make it worse. Tie his arms down," said one voice.

"What's your name? Where did you come from?" said another.

"It looks like he might be coming to again."

"Get the bucket. Get the bucket."

It felt like I was vomiting, or rather, choking on a blue foam that was oozing out of my throat. I kept oozing out this fluid intermittently with splashes of acid from my stomach. Once in a while, I felt a cold rag along my chin wiping off the material. I still couldn't see much through the blur over my eyes, but I could vaguely make out three figures standing over me. Two were by my side and seemed to be trying to take care of me, while a third figure was further away, watching over their actions. As I breathed in, the room had a thick smell of excrement, and the blankets of my bed smelled of filth and sweat.

"Keep coughing it up," one of the voices bade me. Hearing it more clearly, this voice sounded male. He seemed to be holding some sort of bucket underneath my chin.

My arms felt thin and weak; at times, I felt them weakly trying to push away the figures and get me out of the bed. Most of the time, my hands were tied down to the bed I was in. My mind still wasn't clear.

"Sit still. Sit still."

This went on for what seemed like hours—vomiting, coughing up blue foam, being held down. Through out this ordeal, my sight gradually improved, and my mind became clearer. Intermittently, though, exhaustion got the better of me, and I would fall back to sleep.

When I woke up, the entire process happened all over again. I was vomiting less each time, but otherwise, most of the details were the same. In fact, for several days little else happened. I could now tell that the two figures by my side were a man and a woman with another man entering the room periodically as if to supervise. I thought at first, that this was some sort of hospital, but the walls were boarded up with wood and the floor was carpeted. As I looked around the room, it also lacked the various monitors and machines that a medical institution might have. Overall, the room had the appearance of being in an old, run-down house.

After four days, my vision was clear, my mind was coherent, and my stomach was empty enough that I had nothing else to vomit up. I looked over my body and saw a ravaged corpse. I had a sick feeling of nausea as I surveyed my arms and legs. My arms and body were thin and emaciated, except for the parts that were red and edematous from the bite marks that the insects left. My skin itched like a tight hair shirt, and I felt as though I wanted to shed all of it from my face to my feet.

Soon after I woke up that day, I saw a female figure enter the room. She bathed my head with warm water and towels. I asked her, "Where am I?" She didn't answer, but instead left the room to retrieve an older man. The two of them came back in, together.

The older man sat down of my bed and looked at me as though he was familiar with me. "So you're finally waking up."

"Where am I?"

"You're in good hands; you're very lucky to be alive. We found you outside of the city, you would have died or been killed out there on your own."

"This isn't Chesapeake City?" I asked, still dazed.

He smiled, "No, far from it." He spoke with a depth in his voice that carried the sound of authority, but I could tell his tone was more one of concern.

"Where is the city?"

He looked at me as though he was disappointed. "We took you here to save you. You're in a small town far from Chesapeake City. And you're not strong enough to get back. It looked like you must have come through the perimeter of the city, you were badly sick from the insecticide gases."

"Yes. I remember. And the insects? They did this to my skin?"

"I'm afraid so. I'm sorry; we almost found you too late," he said.

"I remember that too… I mean being found."

"Do you think you can drink something? We don't want to push you too fast."

"Yes. Please," I said. "I'm very hungry and thirsty."

The woman left the room as I said this, I hoped she was going to bring me back something to drink. While she was gone, the man told me everything I had done over the past two weeks while I was under their care, about which I remembered very little. Apparently I was quite combative for several days, and I cursed my saviors several times calling them names I was shocked that I used. I was found by the woman who had just left and by another man who had also been by my side for several days. She returned with some broth for me to drink as I listened to the story of how these individuals subsisted in their small community.

I had, throughout my life in Chesapeake City, thought very little of the human civilization that existed outside of the walls of the cities. Unprotected by the fortresses of chemicals and boundaries to the elements, I imagined humans reduced to their most basic and savage behaviors. My opinion had not yet changed. I don't know that it ever did. My experiences outside of the cities would be, though, very clearly divided from my experiences inside. I awakened from my sickened state as a man awakens from a dream. In this case, it was a bad ending to the long dream of my life in Chesapeake City.

The older man, who attended me while I recovered from my chemically induced toxicosis, was Daniel Connors, the leader of a group of individuals who were keeping alive an enclave of a civilization that no longer existed; and he and I became friends. The visions of his group were certainly optimistic, but they weren't utopian by any means. He certainly wouldn't have acknowledged that he was iconoclastic either, and perhaps he wasn't. I learned that his group was comprised simply of the remainders of the human species, left between the new and old cities, who didn't wish to resort to violence to survive.

While some, the affluent, managed to secure a comfortable life in insulated cities, the rest of humanity slipped further into what those living in the new cities clearly saw as social decay. These individuals, though, were like a few hopeful souls lost at sea after all of their companions had abandoned ship. Few populations like this group existed anymore. They lived in pockets here and there, defending themselves from others, satisfied to suffice on the minimal requirements that they could accrue to stay alive.

I was glad that this was the group that I encountered first. In retrospect, I could have found myself in much worse hands. Connors, the apparent leader of the group was reluctant to admit that he was their source of leadership and direction; but I could clearly see how others looked to him for guidance. He seemed strong and powerful; he spoke little, but with conviction in what he said. Even his countenance seemed stern with deep, peering eyes that intently stared back at me while we spoke. I admit there was no one in the cities that I had met who was like him. And I only met perhaps one other person like him in the rest of my travels.

I later learned it was his daughter, Patricia, who found me. The young man who attended me with her, Troy Crossman, was her lover. I suppose would-be husband would be a better phrase to describe him. In a more organized, better-ordered world, they might have been married. Perhaps they were waiting for a moment when they could have seen a better, more secure future to their lives.

Among these three lived a number of others. Usually, the total number of individuals in the community was about fifteen. Some came and went in this community. Some were caught between the anarchy of the outside world, and an envy of the relative comfort and order that they imagined inside the new cities. Some came from far away having heard of Connors' leadership, which they hoped, would give direction to their lives.

For the first week of my stay in this community (at least the first week during which I was conscious), I was too sick and depleted to do much during the day. I began walking with assistance; then with crutches; then with a cane. Connors all along visited me and watched my progress with the occasional word of encouragement. Patricia and Troy were frequently by my side caring for me.

One night, while I was still in this recuperation period, I fell asleep and dreamed that I was back in Chesapeake City, I was at home and in Belinda's arms. Strangely, even in my dream there was something distant in her face. It had already been a long time since I had seen her, but as I recollected her face, it seemed even further than it should have been across the time we had been apart so far. Now that I was outside of Chesapeake City, it seemed to me like a box of people packed tightly together, expanding inside the thin shell stretched across its surface—like a bubble. In my dream, I saw myself as one of those people; the difference was that I was the only person who saw how thin the walls around Chesapeake City were. I awoke saddened, I wanted still to be part of that world, but having seen the world outside, even for the short time that I had been outside, I knew I could never return to the security I felt within the walls of Chesapeake City. I also knew that, however kind Connors and his group had been to me, I was fundamentally an outsider, and also a part of the institution that forced them to live the way they did.

It must have been early morning when I woke up, three or four o'clock. I took my cane and walked outside for a breath of fresh air, to find Connors' tall, thick figure.

"You're not thinking of leaving are you?" He smiled.

"Well, I guess I couldn't make a run for it yet," I said, motioning at my cane.

"I'm not being serious," he said understandingly, "but I wouldn't blame you if you wanted to leave."

"Why?"

"To you, coming from one of the cities, we must seem like savages."

I thought about what he said for a moment. "Can I ask you a question? Do you people resent me at all?"

""You people,'" Connors laughed. "You make us sound like we're a different species."

"I'm sorry," I replied. "I didn't mean it like that."

Connors smiled, "Why would we resent you?"

"I don't know," I said. "I just thought that, since I'm from one of the new cities, and since we live so well…"

"So why aren't you still there now?" he asked.

"It's a long story."

"I don't resent you," he said. "I don't think any of us do. I'm sure if I had it to do over again, I would have chosen to live in the city." Connors didn't seem like a man to carry regrets, so it was hard to believe that he really meant what he said.

"Would you?" I asked.

"Actually, I guess... I don't know. I'm one of the few people who remember what it was like when there was still room for others in the city." He thought for a moment, "I remember it was already so difficult to get into the city, that you felt lucky when you got in and didn't get to the point where you asked yourself if life in the city was right. It seemed like such a mad dash, such a scramble to become one of the elite. I guess that's why I stayed out."

"Actually," I said, "I remember those days too."

"You couldn't possibly, how old are you?" Connors asked me incredulously.

"Older than I look," I replied.

"Really? That old?" He smiled again. "So what are you doing up so early."

"I don't know," I said. "I was just restless, I guess."

"You've spent a long time in bed."

"What are you doing up so early?" I asked.

"There's a lot to be done. I'm just starting my day. The older I get, the earlier I wake up. It give me time to plan the day without being interrupted."

"It seems a lot of people demand your time," I said.

Connors sighed as I said.

"I didn't mean it as an insult."

"I'm old," Connors said. "People don't get to be as old as I am, usually."

"Unless they can survive. So what's your secret?" I asked, half-jokingly.

"That's what everyone wants to know. I guess I've just been lucky. I always wanted to keep my family at a distance from civilization. As things got worse, crime increased. Now, it's harder to survive anywhere in this world." Connors said this and the tone of his voice dropped slightly to a more somber voice that I was more familiar with. "I'm surprised you survived," he added.

"I probably wouldn't have, if Patricia and Troy hadn't found me."

"Even so. Usually someone who is hurt as badly as you doesn't make it. Those mosquitoes you were bitten by—you could have gotten a dozen different diseases," Connors said. "We were all relieved that you were okay."

I felt lucky. I remembered from what I knew of the outside world—that diseases from insect bites were often serious and fatal. Perhaps it was my years in Chesapeake City, during which my immune system was being strengthened by the advanced medicine there, which enabled me to survive now. Perhaps Chesapeake City did give me something to be grateful for after all.

"Well, I should get started on my day. There's a lot to be done," Connors said as he excused himself from the conversation.

Connors didn't seem like the conversational type. He was mostly quiet. In fact, it seemed like he was surrounded by people who wanted him to say more than he did. Maybe that's why he could converse with me more freely. First of all, no one else was around at the time. Second, I didn't have any expectations that Connors should have revolutionary ideologies. I was

grateful that his people had saved me, and I was neither hoping, nor expecting anything more. For me,
though, I remember thinking this was the first conversation I had had in a long while, if not the closest
thing to a conversation.

Connors and I were also roughly the same age;
that may have been one of the reasons we felt closer.
But it also made us irrevocably different. Connors
wore his age heavily engraved in the lines on his face
and in his stern, distant scowl. I was probably older,
but because of the medical treatments I received in
Chesapeake City, I must have looked almost decades
younger than I was. Years ago, I chose to forsake the
natural way of living and aging that Connors was
forced to accept. The years on his countenance were,
for me, a reminder of the life that I didn't choose. I
don't know how much I regretted making my decisions, but I felt like I had an advantage relative to
Connors, and I didn't particularly want to be reminded of that advantage. Connors was at least as
lucky as I was to be alive. He had dodged the violence
of the human civilization he had lived in and the constant threats of illness and disease that the insect
population presented, not to mention that he had been
able to find sustenance in a world that was becoming
increasingly hostile to humanity.

I went back to bed and lay there awake, thinking
about the life that was now more clearly behind me.
It's hard to describe, but since I had come to, I felt
that my mind was becoming clearer—not just because
I had been so physically frail. I was thinking a little
more clearly than I had before. It was a slow change,
and so subtle that I almost didn't realize it was happening.

Chapter IV

Daniel Connors was born in a better world than the one that now surrounded both of us. Unlike me, he was very close with both of his parents. His father and mother both knew that his odds of surviving in the world were becoming increasingly slim as time went on; they saw the inevitable downward slide that the world was on. Also, they were living modest lives; neither had a socially important job, so they knew they had little, if any, chance of making it into one of the new cities.

They debated whether or not to have other children. On one hand, they thought that their child would be safer if he had siblings to protect him. On the other hand, it didn't make sense to bring any more lives into the precarious world they lived in. So their son grew up an only child.

Not too long after his tenth birthday, Connors' parents were killed. They were walking on a dark street too late at night when someone said, "Give me your wallets." They didn't have time to answer or to obey. A peace officer arrived at their house to inform their son of what happened. He stayed only briefly and told young Connors that someone would be back to make arrangement for his future care; his parents had almost no assets or savings built up. There weren't any real foster homes available for children at the time, and the few existing foster homes were unsafe, so Connors was placed in a government and church-operated orphanage.

Even though he could hold his own, Connors was alone; and without a family, he was an easy target for other youths. Connors was never much of a follower, either. He naturally tended to be a loner, but for his own safety, he started hanging out in a small, informal gang. He was tough enough, even at a young age, so that other teenagers didn't mind having him around for additional protection.

By the age of twenty-one, Connors decided to try to get a job as a part of a police force. Most government authorities, including the police, were starting to crumble by this time, but working as a police officer was one of the few jobs that could be had by someone with no training and little education like Connors. Connors didn't like working as part of the police, but it allowed him to make some money and have something of a better life.

Also, working as a police officer was somewhat consistent with the personality that Connors was developing, as he grew older. He saw himself, more and more, as having a responsibility to protect those around him. In a small way, Connors felt that, if he could affect a small sphere of the world around him, by making it safer, then he could achieve some victory against the world that took away his parents. Even then, Connors watched the world around him slowly decay. Crime was increasing, and murder and suicide were becoming more commonplace in the old cities. Most of the affluent and influential were desperately trying to find better lives in the new cities. For some of these people, this was a hopeless endeavor. There really wasn't anyone left to try to improve or develop the old cities, which were becoming centers of urban decay.

Margaret Carter was a municipal official who worked with the police. That's how she met Connors. She was a beautiful young woman with a warm smile, and sometimes when she looked at him and smiled, Connors had an overwhelming desire to protect her happiness from the ugliness of the world that surrounded the two of them.

But her happiness wasn't from a life free of pain. Like Connors, she had her share of hardships at the hands of the cruel world they were both immersed in. She lost her family in a similar way to Connors, and as an attractive, young woman, she was often taken advantage of. As the two got to know each other, the story of her life moved Connors, and he fell in love with her quickly. She, in turn, became very much in love with Connors. She saw strength in his face—the same strength that sustained him during all of his hardships, and she felt safe when she was with him. And for a short while, she was safe with Connors.

After several years together, Margaret and Connors grew increasingly unhappy with their jobs. Because of their professions, they felt trapped in the spiral of urban decay. Neither of them was planning to have children soon, but when Margaret became pregnant, with Patricia, they both considered her to be a blessing. For a short time after her birth, Connors would hold his newborn daughter and be filled with a sense of hopefulness. He wondered, as he looked at her, if she would see an entirely different world when she grew up. He wondered if humanity would return to a life of comfort and material abundance, without the sharp divisions among classes that he knew.

Connors' hopefulness didn't last long, though. Shortly after Patricia's fifth birthday, her mother was killed in another random crime. Connors was devastated by the news, but he tried to be strong for Patricia's sake. He looked into her eyes as she began to understand that her mother was never coming home again, and he remembered how he felt, when he was only five years older than Patricia, and he heard the news about his parents. Connors also felt as though he had failed his wife; he remembered the hope that he had when they met, that he could protect her from the world. Now that Patricia only had Connors left as her family, if he died, she would have an even smaller chance of surviving and would be condemned to the same hardships that Connors faced as a youth or worse.

Not too long thereafter, Connors made the decision to leave the crime and poverty of the city, and he took Patricia with him to find a life away from the new or old cities. In a small way, he thought this might protect her from the threats that he knew were responsible for the deaths of his parents and his wife. Of course, Connors still had to protect Patricia from the insect population, which was even more dangerous in the wilderness, but at least Connors now had only one population to defend himself and his daughter against, instead of two. Connors' idea of a lifestyle away from the rest of civilization appealed to some of the people he knew from the police force, and after a few months, some of them joined him hoping to also find a better life. That's how Connors' clan began to develop.

As time went on, Connors developed better techniques for living off of the land. For instance, he began to move further away from old urban cities, and more toward the perimeters of small towns. Finally he found a community of four or five isolated houses abandoned by their previous residents. This made it easier for his group to get food and shelter. Connors also found it necessary, over time, to develop defenses against gangs who lived on the outskirts of cities and roamed the countryside. A number of violent groups, once the cities were saturated, took to traveling highways and less populated areas to victimize loners or travelers. Though Connors' strategy helped him avoid some of the problems of a more urban world, it was inevitable that crime would eventually spread across the rest of the world.

Connors always carried with him a sense of responsibility. He was, first and foremost, dedicated to Patricia, but as others joined his group, he felt a debt to protect them as well. He lived almost his whole life with the heavy moral obligation to try to protect those around him. Now, close to the end of his life, he was beginning to find that burden more and more onerous.

I was glad that Connors and his group could survive, and I now had them to thank for my life. In their care, my health began to gradually improve. Soon, I no longer needed my cane for walking. I began to explore the outside of the house that I had been staying in, and I started going on walks for further and further distances. Every once in a while, I would wake up a few hours before dawn to talk with Connors. I had come to regard our conversations as quite important. One morning, I spoke to Connors about helping out with some of his tiny agricultural endeavors. He and his group planted small crops and gathered some food from the surrounding wilderness.

"You want to help?" Connors asked.

"Sure," I said. "I'm strong enough."

"You're welcome to, but you don't have to feel like you owe us anything," he said. "We'll be happy if you just keep getting healthier."

"I'd like the activity actually. Consider it rehabilitation for me." Connors smiled as I said this.

"Some of what we eat is just what we grow ourselves," Connors explained. "The rest of it, we get by scouring the area, looking for food."

"And you find enough to feed all the people here?" I asked with surprise.

"So far. It's enough to get by at least. I know it won't be enough to last forever. Soon, we'll have to move on to find enough."

"Where are you planning to go?" I asked.

"Patricia and I have heard that there's some people who are forming sort of a loose colony in the Northwest. Different people have told me similar stories. We can't stay here forever. We're losing more of our food to insects everyday."

"There's not much civilization out there, I guess," I replied.

"I know," he said. "That's the idea. You haven't been with us that long. There are a lot of groups more violent than we are and better able to protect themselves, living in between the cities. The insects, the pollution, the disease— they won't be as thick further away from the cities."

"So you want to move away from the cities?"

"We don't rely on them for anything, and there's no reason for us to stay so close to such a volatile situation." He made a good point, but I didn't want to leave that part of the country. Connors wanted to go further away from what I called civilization; I guess in the back of my mind, I still had hopes of someday returning to one of the new cities, somehow.

"That must be your secret to survival," I said.

"What?"

"You try to move away from the rest of civilization. That makes sense, people are the reason for the problem; if you walk away from the rest of humanity you also walk away from the threats to humanity."

"It's no secret," said Connors. He paused, "As long as we stay out here, an extra pair of hands would always be helpful."

And my hands were helpful for the time that I remained with Connors.

My life had a routine to it when I lived in Chesapeake City. At times, I was unhappy, but my daily work schedule at least lended some stability to my life. With Connors' group, my life again began to fall into a routine. In the mornings, I walked with the rest of the villagers of this tiny utopia—picking leaves and berries as they did. Throughout the day, I would help prepare the food, at night I would eat what little food we had reaped with the rest of them. The meals were often bland or bitter, though, and having been more recently removed from the comforts of civilization, I was less accustomed to the appeal of chewing on leaves, but I was grateful for my life and happy for everything that Connors' band offered me.

My quality of life with Connors' band of followers was intermediate between the comfort I had in Chesapeake City and the adversity I knew I would be experiencing otherwise. Although Connors and his band worked hard to provide for themselves, I never became accustomed to eating food that tasted like paper, or to the feeling of constantly having at least two or three bruises and welts from insect bites on my arms and back. We all wore thick jackets whenever we worked outside, and hoods that covered most of our heads, but many times, the insects could sting my skin through the cloth, and I would get invariably bitten around my face or eyes at least once or twice a day, or more. Regularly, other inhabitants became violently ill as a result of the months of chronic exposure to foods tainted with pesticides and chemicals, or to the toxins produced by the ever-increasing population of insects. Although Connors had found a sustainable niche by wedging himself in between the encroaching city and the expanding pestilence, even he knew that the crack in between the two civilizations was closing around him.

The inhabitants of this village all appeared sickly and chronically ill, but the saddest among them was Leonard, a young man who must have been seventeen years old. He had been living in this narrow existence for several years, and his body was only tenuously hanging on to the narrow trail to adulthood. He was short for his age, and he stood just a little over five feet tall. Despite his short stature, the lanky and wasted appearance of his arms would have made him seem much taller. His eyes were yellow and sunken into his head; beneath them were several layers of dark circles, which gave his face a much older appearance. His skin was retracted and stretched over his body, from the chronic scarring after years of being slowly eaten by the insects of the area. And his speech was slurred. Having been brought up for most of his life in an environment polluted by pesticides and urban toxins, his development had obviously been affected since an early age.

Even though I only interacted with him once or twice, directly, I was curious about what had happened to Leonard during his youth. Once I asked Patricia about his case, while I was collecting leaves with her. "I was working with Leonard earlier today," I started.

"Oh yeah," she replied.

"Yeah. I'm just curious. Did something happen to him?"

"What do you mean?" she asked.

"I don't know. It's just—I've just been noticing that he seems kind of slow. Was he sick as a child or anything?"

"I don't know, I didn't know him back then. We took him in when he was young, his parents were killed years ago, he was brought here by some of the other villagers," she told me.

"I didn't know. How did they pass away?"

"There was a lot of crime and disease where he was, I think they might have been robbed or killed or something. Connors really felt for him."

"That's tragic, this isn't much of a world to grow up in." I didn't realize that in saying this, I had inadvertently offended Patricia's lifestyle. She stopped working and looked up at me.

"It's my world too, you know."

"I didn't mean it that way, it's just that he looks sick and jaundiced. Maybe he has some disease; maybe he needs medical attention someday." I don't know why I suggested this. It was clear to me that, even if someone was ill outside of the cities, that

53

there would be little or no way that they could get medical attention.

I learned only later that Patricia had been hoping to have a child someday with Troy. Perhaps she was in denial of the bleakness of the world she lived in. In my view, the chances of her and Troy being able to bring comfort and a normal life to a child was minimal. What was stranger to me was that she didn't really consider Leonard as disadvantaged and disabled as I did. She knew that he was not as healthy or as clear-headed as he should have been for his age, but perhaps, she had been living with him for so long, that she was no longer as cognizant of his deficiencies. Or perhaps the standard for healthiness that she had grown up with was just different than mine.

"I know," she said in a more understanding tone. "You must look down on our lifestyle, it certainly isn't as luxurious as the life I imagine you had in Chesapeake City."

"We were comfortable," I said with a tone of some guilt.

She looked at me, "Let me show you something."

She took me further east than we usually go to get food, we walked upwards to the top of a hill. "Look at that on the horizon," she said. I looked where she pointed and saw a faint green rim over the horizon.

"Do you see that green cloud in the distance?" she asked. I looked to where she pointed. It looked like someone had sprayed the rim of the horizon with a blurry, green spray paint.

"That green cloud is Chesapeake City—where you came from."

I wasn't surprised.

"Do you see the trees, the vegetation, the green-ery?" she asked.

"Yes."

"Look how the land that way turns from green to brown—look how it gets more barren and empty," she had a tone of conviction as she said this.

I looked instead at the profile of Patricia's face against the landscape of vanishing trees.

"What was it like?" she asked me. "Living there, in Chesapeake City?"

"It's hard to compare it to anything else. I lived there for so long. I've almost forgotten the way I lived before I got there."

"But you know how we live here now," she said.

"It was very utopian… Very clean… No crime, really… Plenty of food." I looked down.

"It sound's like you were happy there."

"I was," I said. "Materially… and for other reasons."

"What happened to make you leave?" she asked. No one in Connors' group had asked me this so far. I imagined it was because they must have felt sorry for me. They probably all suspected that the only reason anyone would leave Chesapeake City would be because they were forced out. In a small way, I was grateful that no one asked me about this. I didn't want to verbally or mentally recap all the things that had happened to me prior to leaving Chesapeake City. In another way, I didn't mind that Patricia did ask. She clearly a bold, young woman.

"Do you want the long story or the short story?" I asked.

"Whichever you prefer," she said.

There was something about the way Patricia asked questions that would have made it difficult to dodge her. She was easy to talk to and had a certain keenness about her that made people she spoke with open up easily.

"Well, I had a hard job." I started. "My work was very taxing. I guess I just couldn't handle it very well, intellectually." I was embarrassed while saying this and looked down. "Then, I was involved with a crime."

Out of the corner of my, eye it looked like Patricia was taken a bit aback by this. "It wasn't entirely my fault," I continued. "There was a couple—a man and a woman—fighting in an alley. I just asked them what was wrong, and, the next thing I knew he and I were coming to blows."

"That's considered a crime?" she asked with a tone of sympathy.

"Well, yeah. Violence isn't well-tolerated in Chesapeake City."

"And for that, they kicked you out?"

"Well, yeah," I answered. "That was part of it."

I felt Patricia's sympathy as we spoke, and I was very grateful for it. This was the first time I had told anyone about what happened to me, and it was nice that Patricia seemed to be on my side.

"I don't even like being this close to it." She looked again towards the distant green hue. "I want to go out to the northwest."

"I know," I said, "Connors—your father, I mean—told me that."

"Yeah," she said. "I've heard of people living out there and doing much better. There's even some fruits and vegetables, or so they say." She had such a hopeful tone as she spoke of the future.

"When I talked to Connors, he didn't seem to think it would be a safe or easy trip."

"I know," she said. "We'll need a lot of luck to make it. Anyone here is welcome to come with. You're welcome to come too." She smiled. "We'll need people who can fight, and we'll need weapons. Troy's going—so is my father, but he is getting older."

I could tell that she knew that the trip wouldn't be a safe one. I wanted to tell her that I would come with her, but in the back of my mind, I still wanted to find a way back to the civilization I knew previously; and her plan was to get further away from it. I could also tell from the tone of her voice that she wasn't going to stay here much longer. She must have looked at her father as old and worn out from his life, and, even though she was grateful for how much he had sacrificed for her, she wanted a better life for herself.

Later in the evening, after most of the others had gone to bed. Connors and I stayed up a little later than the rest. He had to make some further arrangements for their plans to leave soon; and I think he also wanted some encouragement to know that he was making the right decision.

"I want to show you something," Connors said. With this, he took me to the side of one of the houses where we found an old truck. "What do you think?" he asked me.

"Well…" I stammered for a moment. The vehicle was rusted and dented on the outside. The metal parts I could see were so badly corroded that I wondered how they stayed together. "It's…"

Connors could see that I was trying to search for something nice to say. "I know it's no technological marvel," he said, finally ending my discomfort.

I looked at him and we shared a moment's laughter.

"We're going to have to leave soon," Connors continued. "We can't last much longer here."

"I was just getting used to the food, though," I said and smiled. There hadn't been many times in my recent past that I could share a comfortable moment in conversation with someone. I was glad I could with Connors. I didn't usually make attempts at humor in conversation.

"What would you do if we leave here?" Connors asked.

I thought for a moment. "I'm not sure."

"You know you're more than welcome to come with us if we leave."

I smiled at this. "Thank you," I said.

We talked for only a few minutes longer before a swarm of mosquitoes surrounded us. We quickly said our good-byes for the night and rushed back to our rooms.

That night, I stayed up late trying to convince myself that I should go with the rest of Connors' band on their trip. I knew that I had a better chance of survival with them than on my own, and I knew that I could live the rest of my life with Connors' band more comfortably; and, at least have food and shelter in one form or another. Still, though, I felt that I wasn't a part of this group, and I couldn't ignore my desire to return to one of the new cities someday, no matter how unrealistic that prospect was. It took me, in fact, many weeks of staying with Connors and his group for me to realize that my hopes of returning to Chesapeake City someday were unrealistic. Maybe this was something I knew all along, but it wasn't until after my most recent conversation with Patricia that I actually admitted it to myself.

Although I admitted that the odds of returning to Chesapeake City were low, that night, my thoughts again turned to my hope of joining one of the other new cities. The only way that I could return to one of the modern cities like Chesapeake City would be to find one of the old cities, those that were the crumbling remnants of what civilization was once like. Only there, would I be able to find some infrastructure and perhaps the remnants of a government, to which I could appeal my case and request a return to the new cities.

As I drifted to sleep, I also noticed something else. Throughout my stay with Connors' community, I was beginning to think more clearly. Early on, I felt like my thinking was clouded, but recently, I was more lucid, more alert. At the time, I attributed these changes to the ordeal I went through when I left Chesapeake City; certainly it must have been at least a day or so that my lungs were saturated with pesticides that must have clouded my thinking. I thought to myself, I must still be recovering from my exposure to those chemicals. I remembered as I thought back further, the way I felt lethargic and malaise while I was in Chesapeake City. Reflecting on this, I soon fell asleep.

I slept for two, maybe three hours, when I was awakened by the sounds of engines and of feet running quickly through grass and dirt outside. Since I had been with Connors' group, though, I hadn't seen a single car. I quickly put on my shoes in a half-awake daze while I heard the sounds of men's voices; they sounded threatening—they were the sounds of a mob. Two men broke into the door of my room, just as I was about to open the door. One pushed me down to the floor while the other stood over me and started hitting me with a large stick that he used like a baseball bat. I was lucky to think fast, and I collapsed to the floor saying, "Oh God please don't hurt me. Take whatever you want."

Thinking that they had gotten the better of me, the would-be captors stopped beating me, and moved to lift me up off the floor. It was long enough for me to plan what to do next. As the one with the bat put his other arm over me, I quickly twisted forward and pulled the bat out of his hand as I rose to my feet. While the other was moving toward me, I had enough time to swing once at the first man. I felt his cheek bone crush on the other end of the bat. It would be a second or two before he would attack again.

The other man was armed with a chain, I pulled back the bat as if to swing at him. As he ducked to get out of it's way, I jabbed forward with the bat two times catching him once in the face and once underneath his chin. I turned as the first man was getting back to his feet and caught him across the top of his head. As he fell to the ground, I hit him a second time with the bat down over his head. I had hoped that he would be unconscious now. As I finished the blow, the other attacker hit me in the head with his chain. I swung around again to retaliate, but he caught my ribs with a second blow. Before he could strike a third time, I hit him hard in his right arm; that at least disabled him for a while. I continued swinging at his face and at his arms as he tried to protect myself, until I got the better of him.

These were not old men; they were much younger than I was, but they looked sickly and aged. I realized this as I continued hitting this other man over his head, and after a couple more blows, he too was on the ground. Before I did much else, I heard the sound of more fighting outside, which I hadn't noticed while I was being attacked. I rushed outside to see Troy and Leonard standing back-to-back fighting off others. Other men in our camp were holding their own as well, including Connors who was grabbing one or two at a time, and beating them badly. Watching him fight was impressive, and he was throwing some of these men around like rag-dolls.

Troy had his hands full with an attacker, who looked like he was among the most agile of the group. Leonard, in the meantime, was being beaten by one of the attackers who caught him in the head with a steel rod. As Leonard fell to the ground, I rushed his attacker with my bat and swung twice, connecting through his head both times.

Another man, a member of Connors' band was being rushed by one of the attackers. The attacker had some sort of device that sent out electrical shocks, and he stunned the member of Connors' band. Quickly, I ran to take him on, while he was distracted using this device. I easily swung at him and momentarily knocked him out from behind.

Two more ended up hitting me from behind. One of them swung at my legs and knocked me off balance; the other swung with a pipe and grazed the top of my head while I fell. Connors, who was picking off other men with relative ease, was swinging a six-foot staff of wood, and picked off each of my attackers. I looked at him in the eye as if to say, thank you, but we both turned our attention to other attackers.

Troy had been caught from behind by another attacker, who was holding him by the arms while another man swung a chain at him. I was able to knock out the man holding him, freeing him to launch a punch at the man with the chain. I ended up fighting off some of the other attackers as I stood alongside Troy. We seemed to be defending ourselves well, when a truck full of other men began circling. The attackers ran off and jumped into the first truck as a second truck drove straight through the crowd.

Troy, who had a knife, bravely ran after the second truck, maybe with the intention of cutting its tires, but he fell just short of the rear bumper as it drove off. Connors rushed quickly behind Troy, and the two of them walked back to the rest of us as the trucks drove away. I realized, only then, how fast my heart was beating. A thousand questions rushed through my mind: Who was this gang? What did they want? Why did they come into the wilderness to find an isolated community just to fight?

As Connors and Troy walked back to the rest of us, Patricia ran outside, apparently looking for Troy. They embraced each with some relief that the other was relatively unharmed. Then Patricia turned her attention to her father before inquiring about the

rest of us. As the adrenaline began to wear off, I
realized how badly I had been hurt. Others looked
hurt as well. Connors and Troy, on the other hand,
looked remarkably unscathed, though they did the
lion's share of the fighting.

I felt a pinch in my shoulder and realized it was
some sort of mosquito as I swatted it off. Gradually,
I became more aware of the insects in the air. Connors spoke up, "This is a bad hour to be outside.
Let's all head back inside; we can take care of our
injuries tonight, and find out what's missing tomorrow." Other members of the camp, who were obviously shaken by what had happened, surrounded
Connors. Patricia was assessing the injuries of each
person as she contained her own emotions. I ended
up walking back inside along Troy.

"Who were they?" I asked him.

"Just another gang. This has happened before.
They just come to raid us, trying to find food or
hidden stashes or anything valuable."

"Is this the same group?"

"No. I don't think so, it's hard to remember
what the last group looked like."

I looked at some sort of insect that had landed
on Troy's arm. He smacked it cursing.

"By the way," he said, "thanks for your help."
He held open the door to one of the buildings as I
walked through the doorway.

"Sure," I said. "I mean... That's the least I could
have done. You're a good fighter."

"You, too." Troy looked at me with his clear
blue eyes full of youth, and his head covered by a
crop of brown, curly hair. Looking at him, I juxta-
posed the faces of the men who had attacked us.
They looked old and weak; I wasn't surprised that

they weren't much of a match for Troy. I thought how surprising it was that Troy had survived without suffering the same aging effects of his lifestyle. On the other hand, he was one of the younger members of the community. Still, for a moment, looking at Troy was like looking at the next generation, and I was, momentarily hopeful about humanity's future, the ordeal I had just been through not withstanding.

"Why did they come here to fight us?" I asked.

"They're just poor and hungry. I don't know if you noticed, but only a few of them were fighting, most of them were going through our houses scavenging while the others kept us busy. Some gangs live out in the wilderness, others stay in some of the older cities, or what's left of them." He looked thoughtful for a moment. "You must really miss Chesapeake City, now."

I did, but I didn't want to admit that to him. "This is a hard life."

"Yeah, I know. Patricia, I mean, everybody here, wants to leave. You know, we're thinking of moving further away."

"She's told me," I said. "Connors did too."

We were talking outside of the door of the room where I slept. Connors walked by and put his hand on my shoulder, "You fought very well, both of you. I'm glad you're all right."

Troy looked up at Connors with a countenance that said, "What is to be done?"

Seeing the fear in Troy's face, Connors responded. "I know. We can't stay here much longer."

"I've had enough of a night. I'm going to go to bed," said Troy.

"That's a good idea," said Connors, "get your rest for tomorrow."

"What's tomorrow," I asked.

"That gang you just saw—there are gangs out there that are plenty worse. We were lucky this time. We're lucky to be alive."

"You're thinking of leaving sooner than later," I wondered.

Connors started to walk off. "I'll let you get your rest. We've got a long journey ahead of us; maybe I should stop putting it off."

The next day, I awoke with a throbbing in my head. I felt the lump that was the source of my pain, which I hadn't remembered being there the night before. I strained to get out of bed, and realized my left hand was also pretty swollen. The adrenaline in my system from the fight must have blunted my body's pain response. I left my room and surveyed the camp, now realizing how severe the damage was. Most of the windows on the houses had been broken in; barrels of water were spilled; some of our supplies of food were missing, the rest was dumped over, and insects were beginning to swarm over the exposed food. Patricia and Troy were already awake, and were trying to fight off the insects, but they were mostly just getting bitten and stung. Finally, Patricia walked away in frustration and began to cry. Connors, seeing that the food was wasted, walked over to the pile and set it on fire. I walked over to him.

"We shouldn't have had so much food, anyway," Connors said as he watched the fire slowly grow from a distance. "When you stockpile that much food, you're attracting insects and gangs." I saw the sadness in his eyes.

"Maybe things will be better, when you all get wherever you're going," I knew my words wouldn't comfort him much.

"You're not coming with us?"

"I don't know. I didn't realize you'd be leaving so soon."

"That's okay. You're just used to having a different lifestyle, and you'll never be able to have it with us. But you might not be able to find it anywhere." He paused, "and you may die searching for it."

"Neither of us have much of a prospect for the future," I said. Immediately after I said this, I was regretful for potentially insulting Connors' plan.

"I just want to stay put. I want to find a place where I won't get chased away," Connors said. "Every time something like this happens, it's a reminder to me. It reminds me that I'm just holding on to whatever threads of survival I can grasp."

"It's a precarious way to live," I agreed.

"It's a hard way to live, and I'm too old to keep living it."

Instead of repairing all the damages, everyone in the camp spent most of the next few days packing up their things. Connors didn't have to announce that they would be leaving; they all seemed to know on their own. I saw Patricia later that day, she was quiet and somber; the previous day was especially hard on her. Connors had a large truck and some gasoline he had been saving. The villagers all piled their things on board, and then climbed in. They looked like a strange band; each was wearing his or her jacket, with their goggles and thick gloves.

Patricia and Troy said their goodbyes to me.

"You're crazy for not coming with us," Troy said.

"I know... maybe, so," I said.

"Take care of yourself." Patricia wished me well and hugged me goodbye. She hugged me as a gesture of friendship, but it had been a long time since I had been close to a woman.

Connors didn't say much when he said goodbye to me. He had always been a man of few words, even though he spoke the most to me. I could see, though, that he was, at least, somewhat saddened by the fact that we were parting ways. Deep down, there was probably also some pity in his look. I don't think he thought he would ever see me alive again. In retrospect, I would have thought the same thing. Most of the people from the camp must have thought that I was crazy for trying to make it on my own. It wouldn't be until later that I would realize the irony in that.

Once Connors' group was gone, I had to make my preparations to leave as well. Gathering from what they left behind, I took whatever I could to make myself better prepared to face the outside world. Over the time I had been staying with the camp, I had gathered some clothing, including some protective gear that I wore while I was working outdoors. There was some food left, too, although, it wasn't enough for me to survive on for very long.

I wasn't sure why I stayed behind. I had felt my mind becoming clearer while I was staying with Connors and his camp, but I still felt my judgement was sometimes clouded. I realized this more in retrospect, but my decisions somehow still didn't yet seem rational to me. I wouldn't until later learn why my thoughts were so clouded.

Perhaps, though, I also couldn't yet accept that I would never again live in a modern city. I remember when I first was found by Connors' camp. They all seemed so dirty and unkempt to me. It seemed silly after what I had been through, but I found myself looking down on them. The days of working outside in the heat wearing several layers of thick clothing made the members of the camp sweaty and smelly, and the grease and dirt was thick on their skin. As these changes progressed in my appearance as well, I gradually became less cognizant of the how unclean the others were, but I still remembered this initial impression.

On the other hand, in some ways, I wished I could have seen myself as a part of Connors' group. I recollected the people that I knew in Chesapeake City: Dr. Adler, Belinda. Looking back on them now, they all seemed so unreal, and my daily interactions with them seemed like dreams. I remembered going through the motions of daily life when I lived at Chesapeake City, but each day now ran together in my memories, nothing stood out differentiating one day, week, or month from another. By way of contrast, everyone in Connors' camp was much more "real". Troy had a specific earnestness about him; Patricia was a multi-faceted person capable of experiencing real emotion; Leonard even seemed capable of an emotional depth that I didn't even think I could have obtained. That was what made me so different than the rest of Connors' group. I felt that I was like the citizens of Chesapeake City, existing on a TV screen while these people were three-dimensional.

I'm not sure if my judgements about the citizens of Chesapeake City were true. I was looking back through a memory that was more hazy than focused. I didn't know if my assertions that the members of Chesapeake City were two-dimensional were based on reality, or on the weakness of my memory and my inability to focus on their identities as individuals. Regardless, I knew what I was then and there, and I knew that my identity was less "real" than the identity of the other villagers.

All these thoughts and others came to me that night, the last night that I would spend in Connors' former camp. As a denouement to the time I spent with Connors and his village, I decided to spend the remainder of that night in the camp. Connors' group had the advantage of a vehicle for travel. I thought it would be a better idea for me to wait until morning to have a full day's light.

That morning, I covered myself in a thick jacket, gloves, and goggles, and walked away from the camp. Even as I awoke, I immediately felt regret and uneasiness over not joining Connors and his group. I might have even considered continuing off in their direction, but there was little chance that I would make it to wherever they had gone. I was now, once again, alone in my travels.

Chapter V

At first, I decided to walk northward; I knew there were other advanced cities in that direction, like New Toronto, Bay City, and Jefferson City. I had hoped to walk along the patches of vegetation and wilderness—between the crime and social decay of the old cities, and the chemical clouds outside of the new cities. By keeping close to whatever patches of vegetation that I could find, I could ensure a constant, if sparse food supply and a degree of shelter. As I learned, the latter would not be easily afforded to me.

Almost every time I lay down to sleep, the sting of a passing insect awakened me. Whenever I lay down, I tried to cover myself in the thick clothing and jackets that Connors had given me, but whatever part of me was exposed, my face or my lips, would be invariably pricked at by the ubiquitous insects. As I pushed on further, I became more and more deprived of sleep or rest. The sleep deprivation I suffered not only made me uncomfortable, but also made me less able to protect myself in the few moments when I could get sleep. I needed to sleep lightly, but my body found the deprivation of rest unbearable, and I found myself falling into a deeper and deeper sleep whenever I lay down, and a more disoriented mental state whenever I awakened.

One morning, a large beetle woke me up, scraping at the inside of my nostril. I should have felt it on my face sooner. I woke up frantically trying to claw it out. The more I tried to grasp it, though, the more tightly it wedged itself inside my nose. After a matter of seconds, I began clawing at my nose and beating at the side of it; I found that this only aggravated the insect more, and I felt it poking through the skin of my nasal septum. I didn't realize how finely the rest of my body was triggered by this stimulus in my nose, and the right side of my body started twitching uncomfortably and uncontrollably. As the insect burrowed its way further into my nose, the seconds stretched out in time. I grabbed one of the tools from my bag and poked at the insect penetrating the skin on the side of my nose. I thrust again, this time more forcefully; and the insect began flailing in pain. I could feel each of its extremities beating rapidly; as my nose filled with goo, I knew I had at least injured this insect. I began to turn the point of the instrument downward to push this beetle outside of my nose, until I could grab it by its rear. Unfortunately, it must have attached itself to the skin of my nose, and I felt intense pain as I pulled the insect out with a firm yank.

I stomped on it several times, but its limbs remained motional, whirling in tiny circles. The insects were becoming much more robust as they evolved. Even after it must have been dead, I continued stomping at the insect in a vain attempt to punish it for how much I had suffered. Only afterward, did I wipe off the blood, my own and the insect's, that was dripping out of my nose and along the side of my nose from out of the hole I had punctured.

On another morning, I awoke to the sensation of fine, prickling pins and needles rising up my legs to my inner thighs and my perineal area. As I rubbed my legs the pricking sensations became more intense and painful. In my half-awake daze, I quickly figured out what was going on. I stood up and ripped off my pants to see hundreds of spidery ants crawling around my legs and groin. I clawed at my own legs inflicting more damage to myself probably, than to the insects, but I had no choice. As my lower extremities were exposed, I was swarmed by mosquitoes, which began draining the blood from my legs. My own fingers were tearing at my skin, and I was now openly bleeding. I remembered another useful item in my bag from Connors and I pulled out a bottle of alcohol astringent, and began rubbing it on my legs as I swatted away the mosquitoes and picked the ants off my skin. I felt like I had spent a half-an-hour pulling bugs off of my skin before I finally decided I was able to put my pants back on, and I felt my tender skin rubbing against the inside of the cloth. There were no remaining ants on my skin, but I could still feel the sensation of their tiny limbs and painful stings as I walked away. Every movement I made chafed the wounds on my tender skin.

In between incidents like these, I thought of Delinda. I wondered if she knew how much I was suffering. She always told me that her love for me would be eternal, like any good wife should, and part of me still thought this was true, but only a small part of me. Unconditional love is hard to come by—maybe impossible. I don't mean to sound pessimistic, but I was living in a very painful world. It was hard to believe that something as beautiful as unconditional love could co-exist on the same, ugly planet that I was living on. Besides, if unconditional love ever did exist, it probably wasn't something that Belinda and I shared.

Most of the time I spent though, wasn't quite as bad as this; I was uncomfortable, but I now had lower expectations of what comfort was. Strangely, these events didn't make me regret my decision to leave Connors' band. They did make me realize that this wilderness was no longer my domain. As a human, I had acceded my right to it to the more evolved insects. Humanity once felt that insects were merely a nuisance. As insects evolved and multiplied, they became something to be controlled. Now, from the perspective of the new cities, the insects were a territorial influence, encroaching on the geographic domain of humans. I felt differently about these beasts, though. By all rights, they had a better claim on the globe than I did. They were outliving, out-smarting, and out-evolving human society. I realized I didn't belong in this wilderness, and I never wanted more to return to Chesapeake City.

I felt another sentiment, though. As much as I hated that the insects were capable of attacking me, most of the time, I wanted them to win. I wished they were able to kill me swiftly with one gesture, rather than slowly draining my energy and my body with their incessant presence and repeated attacks. My death in this environment was inevitable; I knew I was dying, but I wanted my death to be less painful and less slow; the insects around me were taking apart my body virtually cell by cell.

My travels in the wilderness lasted weeks, but eventually my desire to retreat back to a human society took hold. I knew I would be unable to quickly get back into the modern cities, but I now hoped to at least enter one of the old cities. Though I knew in the old society, crime, violence, and the elements of social decay would threaten me, I at least knew that these would all be threats posed by other humans. Certainly, the humans living in the old cities were more comfortable than I was in the wilderness. Moreover, it had been weeks since I had contact with another mammal, much less a human being. The humans I did see, roaming the highways, in bands, looked like the gang that had attacked Connors' village; and I knew it wouldn't be safe to make contact with them.

With my resolution to return to the cities, I felt more comfortable. At the beginning of this journey, I fought off my insect attackers with more fury, and I made more efforts to prevent their attacks; but now, I was becoming despondent with the knowledge that even my best efforts wouldn't be enough anyway. Perhaps this was because I realized that, in the end, the insects would probably beat me as well as the rest of humanity, no matter what we did. Another part of me was becoming more comfortable with the notion of my death. It was too much effort to try to stay alive in such a hostile environment. One night I went to sleep cursing, for the first time, the medical treatments that prolonged my life. It was a momentary lucidity only, and I quickly shook off my suicidal ideations, but these notions made me realize how detached and weakened my will to live had become. I thought also of Connors. He had lived in this environment much longer than I had, and I imagined that, if I were living his life, the suicidal urges which were just now beginning to grasp me would have long since become irresistible.

When I briefly thought of Belinda, it seemed I could think of her more clearly now, although the memory of her was still hazy. I wondered what she must have been doing in Chesapeake City, and I longed for the warmth and comfort that I knew when I lived with her. I didn't miss her; in fact, I now could see clearly that I missed the material comfort of Chesapeake City rather than her company; but I did envy her and the life that I had lost access to.

I was now, I judged, closer to the old cities, and I felt that I could reach one within a few days' travel. The closest city to me was Newark, New Jersey. I walked until I found a highway that would lead to Newark, and I began walking parallel to it, but a few meters away—near enough that I could keep the road in sight, but far enough away from it so that I would not be seen by travelers.

Newark rose on the horizon with a brown and gray haze hanging above it. I could almost feel the depression in the city's presence as I approached it, and I instantly became sorry for heading this way. But I was tired, it had been weeks since I slept for a full night, and I had long since forgotten the taste of tolerable food. Although I once looked down on the food that Connors and his band ate, I would have welcomed any change in my diet from the raw leaves I had been chewing and sucking on for sustenance.

As I neared the edge of the city, the vegetation began to thin out. I had to make my decision to proceed and hope that I could find food and refuge once I was in the city, which would be by nightfall. Walking alone, as the fields around me grew progressively emptier, I felt more vulnerable to the elements. I passed through one area of abandoned farming land. The dirt in its fields was nicely organized into rows, but overgrown with weeds and minimal grass. I thought of how long it must have been since these fields were cared for, back when it wasn't such a futile effort to try to supply food to a nearby city.

I was trying to walk quickly to Newark, out of anxiety or desperation. If I had thought more about what would likely happen to me in Newark, I might not have proceeded so hastily. I might have stayed at the outskirts of the city, or stayed outside the city entirely until the next day, but I wasn't thinking. Perhaps I was driven to continue by a deeper longing to be with other humans. Perhaps I thought I could find shelter—that there would be safety in numbers. I even felt some hopefulness as I walked—perhaps it was relief at the prospect of rejoining human society. I moved closer to the highway as Newark neared.

As I predicted, by nightfall, I was within the outskirts of the city. As I neared the city's center, more figures passed me—some staring, some laughing, some unaware of me. It felt strange to be within the midst of a civilization again, especially one so unfamiliar. I felt as though I had been isolated for years. Moreover, I would have thought that my presence would have drawn more attention as well. Having just spent several weeks in the wilderness, I was bearded, ungroomed, unkempt, and dirty, but to my surprise, I almost blended in.

I remembered the old cities I knew during my youth, before I lived in Chesapeake City. There were pigeons and rodents, both of which freely roamed the streets, scavenging the plentiful food that was discarded by their human co-inhabitants. As I looked around the streets of Newark, I saw no creatures other than insects and humans. And the insects I saw in the city were different from what I encountered previously; there was a great diversity of insects in the wilderness—diversity in size, shape, and color of each insect, but all the insects in the city all seemed similarly small and black. There were small black flies swarming around waste heaps and garbage piles, and there were small black ants covering the street. The latter were so numerous, that I thought they might overtake me if I paused to sit down or rest. So I kept walking.

I had hoped that I could have found some food, perhaps in a store of some sort, though I had no money; perhaps, more realistically, in discarded trash. The streets were devoid, though, of any businesses. They were lined instead, on either side, with large empty buildings that looked like abandoned warehouses. Many of these building were just skeletons made up of rafters and planks, and you could look through them to the next street. In each building, there were a number of flames burning, with vaguely human shadows crouched around them.

Every few blocks, there might be a group of people standing and talking, mostly in the shadows. There were dim, electrically-powered lights, which were too weak to illuminate the city at night. I remembered my late-night walks through the streets of Chesapeake City—how the streetlights almost made the night as bright as day.

I continued walking to the center of the city, but it was getting late, and I began seeing fewer and fewer other humans. Though I was hungry, I decided to abandon my search for food temporarily. I walked past the remains of a building; it looked like it had been burned or otherwise damaged, and only a scaffold remained standing. There was no door, so I walked inside. As I moved around on the first level, I could hear my feet brushing through the sand and dirt on the floors. There was a stench occupying the building that was almost overpowering, but I thought it wiser to stay inside rather than take my chances on the streets in the dark. Besides that, I was tired.

As I awoke, there was a group of gray-silver bugs huddled around one of my legs. At first it was difficult to even see them since they were the same color as the dust on the floor, but the deep pricks of their bites woke me up quickly. I swatted them off my leg as they darted up into my pants. I had long since learned to cover myself completely before I slept, but in this case, they must have found a small entrance into my clothing. Once again, I found myself trying to tear off my clothing, but not being able to work fast enough.

Finally, as I shook off the tiny beasts, I became conscious of a skeleton of a figure staring at me through the doorway of the room that I was in. He looked at me through sunken eyes, which were buried under the wrinkles of his face and the few strands of thin hair, which hung down over them. Looking at him, I thought that he might collapse and die at any moment. As I became aware of him he continued to stand staring at me, without relieving me of the burden of his heavy gaze. I began to put my clothes back on before I attempted to engage him in conversation. After all, he might have been a madman, and I didn't want to accidentally provoke anger. On the other hand as I looked at him, I realized that this was the most meaningful bit of human contact I had had in almost a month, and I decided to try talk to him. He seemed too frail and weak to do me any harm anyway.

"Hello? Who are you?" I approached him slowly as if he were a wild animal that I didn't want to frighten. As I moved closer, though, he showed no signs of fear, and continued peering at me with a determined gaze. "I haven't been in Newark long." My words were clumsy and awkward. I realized it had been a long time since I had even spoken aloud.

As I took another step, he pulled back his coat, revealing a crude-looking metal box with an opening in the front. In another instant a small object flickered in the gray-tinged sunlight. I felt it hit my arm and it jolted me as I fell to the ground. Stunned as I was, in moments I felt his tiny hands scavenging in the pockets of my pants, which I had been holding up, but which now fell back down around my ankles. He darted over to my bag and quickly sorted through its contents removing anything he thought might be valuable. A moment later, he darted out the doorway peeking back at me one last time before leaving the room. I wasn't sure why he turned back around to look at me, but there was no hint of regret in his eyes. My entire body started to tingle before the sensation came back. I shook myself off and noticed the tiny silver beetles regrouping around my leg. This time I shook them off less vigorously. I was somewhat discouraged by my last encounter. And resisting these little insects, who so badly wanted me out of their territory, seemed useless in the long run. Many of the possessions, which he had taken, had enabled me to defend myself, travel, and survive outside the cities. Now, my pockets were empty and my remaining possessions were the clothing on my back. I was still hungry, and the skin on my legs was beginning to blister and peel, probably from the toxins released by the tiny gray insects.

When I finally left the building, I realized the sun was hanging midway in the gray sky, leading me to guess that it was mid-afternoon. The city seemed even more frightening in the light as I saw the humans around me. The inhabitants all had an ashen color to their skin, which seemed thin and just barely able to cover their bodies. A few had bright red abscesses and boils on their faces. They were covered in scars and defects in their skin, probably from years of being slowly eaten by insects. Others were almost completely naked and lying in the streets. Their limbs were wasted and thin—tapering off to a withered point. Still others looked thick and doughy; their skin seemed swollen with edema, to the extent that their eyes were halfway closed. Though my newly acquired survival skills had helped me survive in the wilderness, they would be of no use to me here.

I felt as though I was the only color character in a black and white movie. Though I was dirty enough to blend in, the green stains on my pants from the wilderness and the pink color of my flesh gave me away as an outsider. Hopeless as I was, I realized the gravity of my decision to come to Newark, and now that I had lost many of my few remaining possessions, I didn't think I could have returned to the wilderness and survived. I faced the day with a bleak immediate future; I was still hungry and tired, and now I had lost valuable resources. Worse, I was largely stranded in Newark now.

I walked back out in the streets to resume my search for food, but I realized how scarce it had become. As I passed others, I felt like I was more "in tact" as a human being, despite all that I had been through, and I felt a pity for those around me. As I looked into their glazed, empty eyes, I realized how much further along they were than I in the path that we were sharing together. The same forces that were forcing these people out of their evolutionary niche in the world were now beginning to take their toll on me. I still had a glimmer of hope that my future would be better, but the condition of the people I saw all around me portended a worse outcome.

I thought perhaps that I could find another area in the city that was not as ravaged as where I was. But the city streets were like a maze to me, and eventually, I was so deep into the wasted city that it seemed like it stretched out all around me without end. Yet those around me must have been getting some sort of sustenance from somewhere. As I persisted I found some local businesses. I happened upon a location that was selling food. A large truck under heavy guard was making a delivery of some bread and produce. The front of the restaurant was heavily sprayed with pesticides, and the scent reminded me of the pesticides I breathed in when I was leaving the perimeter of Chesapeake City. Even though I had no money and was nauseated by the chemical odor, I went inside to find long lines and a sparse supply of goods. I contemplated stealing some food somehow, but the building was too well-guarded.

Outside of the store, there was another congregation of individuals a block away. I decided to walk up to them just to join the crowd. In the center was a small truck with a group of three men who were selling a fine white powder. The prices that the crowd was paying for this commodity were extraordinary. People were offering money or bartering what looked like valuable possessions. The men and their truck seemed a little out of place in this setting. The truck seemed too modern and advanced for the relatively poor and dirty environment. I must have drawn attention to myself by being so quiet and motionless while the rest of the crowd was jostling together for attention. Finally one of the three men turned to me and asked me, "And what will you offer us for your concentrate?"

I answered without thinking, "If I had any money, I would spend it on food."

The three men seemed angered by my response, and one of them moved at me. He was much larger and more physically imposing than any of the others in the group or even any in the crowd. "Don't like concentrate, eh? If you take your concentrate, you won't need food, friend." With this, he produced a sleek steel bar and swung it at my head as he started moving toward me. I thought I could have taken most of the other men there, but against him, I decided I would do better to take a few steps back, especially since I hadn't eaten since the previous day. He persisted, and followed me, though. I moved back, until he felt he had chased me away.

One peculiar thing I remembered was the way he called me "friend." He said it with a peculiar emphasis as though he knew something about me. I thought of these things as I walked away.

I was still hungry, though, and I decided I would do better to stay nearby this store. First, this was the only place I had found food since I had been in Newark. Second, I thought I would be somewhat safe in the crowd—that the presence of so many people might deter further attacks on me like the one in the abandoned building.

There was another part of the crowd standing around the entrance to this store, trying to panhandle the passers-by. Though I hoped I would never stoop this low, I was hungry and desperate, and so I joined this crowd with the faint hope of being tossed a mouthful of food. Most of the others were more aggressive than I, and they abrasively approached each of the individuals who were gathered there to buy food. Most of the crowd was swatted away by the store's security, like a swarm of gathering insects. At times, I tried to say something to someone coming out with an armful of food. Usually, though my voice was drowned out by the pleas from the rest of the crowd. When a more generous person walked out, they often flung food away quickly and randomly, probably in the hope of diverting the crowd's attention away from them. When this happened, a few members of the crowd started aggressively butting together to get as close as possible to the food. I was usually on the periphery.

Later in the afternoon, I was still without food. One of the taller men in the crowd was also pan handling. He had a long, thin face, which accentuated his hunger. He seemed to be a little more adept at reaching over the rest of the crowd to grab food. In one instant he grabbed what seemed to be an entire handful. He turned to walk away to eat his food, when he passed me saying, "Here, come with me," in a quiet tone. He put his hand on my shoulder as he passed me.

"What's your name?"

I told him.

"Looks like you're having some bad luck," he said as he looked down at me. I thought about how bad I must have appeared to earn his pity among so many obviously unfortunate people. I felt somewhat scolded by his remark, but his expression indicated that he didn't mean any harm.

"Listen, my name is Jonas. Here." With that, he handed me some food. For a moment, I looked at him with some disbelief. "Go ahead," he reassured me.

"Thank you," I said. "Thank you." I could feel that my tongue was weak from disuse and hunger, and my words came out awkwardly. "Don't you need this food for yourself?"

"Yeah," he replied. "But I'll probably eat a couple of times what you eat, anyway. Really I don't mind." My mouth watered as I salivated in anticipation of eating the food in my hands. "Listen. It looks like you're probably new at this. Try to watch what I do. I'll help you out if I can."

Most of that day passed, and I was still hungry, but at least there was some food in my belly. Moreover, each bite was amazingly filling. At the end of the day, Jonas gave me a couple more bites of food. I felt like a fool living in this environment that I knew nothing about, so I followed Jonas as he walked away—my mind filled with questions I hoped he could answer.

More than ever, though, I felt stranded and alone. It can be an ugly feeling to not feel cared about, and even the small feeling of caring and comfort that Belinda gave me was more than what I had now. Feeling more lucid even though I was hungry and weak, I could now feel how little she truly cared about me. Now—on my own, in Newark—there was no one who cared about me at all. I knew I was just another face polluting the world with my humanity. It seemed strange to me that at the brink of our extinction—the time when all of humanity needed most to band together and fight for survival—we were now the most divided against each other. I thought of the world I once knew. In that world, the people around me now might have been well-respected professionals—perhaps engineers or doctors. I thought about how much they would have, in that circumstance, purported to care about each other. But now, in this place and time, each person's self-interests were unmasked by their neediness. I guessed that was what we'd all been reduced to, myself included. I would soon come to realize how true this observation was.

Walking and talking with Jonas, though, made me feel unusually happy. Just exchanging words casually with someone else seemed very precious now, and I felt very content to share even very few words with him as though we were friends.

"You're very kind to help me," I said.

"That's alright. I've had help from people in my life too."

"I can't imagine surviving to be your age in an environment like this." Jonas chuckled as I said this. I realized how tactless a statement it was. "I didn't mean it as an insult," he added. Jonas wasn't that old at all, but he was much older than most other people in the city were. And those people who were older were sickly and near-death.

"I've had struggles," Jonas said, "maybe some close calls. I've gotten lucky. I'm good at snatching food."

"What was that 'concentrate' that those men were selling?"

"Wow," Jonas said, "You're really not from here." He chuckled a little again. "Where did you come from?"

"I don't know if you would believe me if I told you."

"Try me", Jonas replied.

I told Jonas the story of what had happened to me quickly. Rushing through it, trying to summarize it in a few sentences, it almost seemed like a distant dream. At first, I thought Jonas must have thought I was crazy, rambling about my former life as a researcher in one of the new cities. I heard myself and almost even doubted my own veracity as I told the story, but as I added details, I could tell that Jonas was starting to believe me. Jonas was a very good audience, though, and he seemed to be curious about every detail of my life. I imagine that it must have astonished him to hear about life in the new cities, and my stories were probably the closest thing to a look into the new cities that he had ever gotten.

"I know it all must sound hard to believe," I said.

"No... well... sort of. Tell me more about Connors."

"He was a giant of a man," I said. As I said this, I again felt a tinge of regret for not staying with Connors and his band. I wasn't sure what, up until this point, kept me from regretting not going with Connors. Perhaps I was too preoccupied with my other problems like getting food and staying alive to even think about it. I could tell by his expression that Jonas was as impressed hearing about Connors as I was when I knew Connors.

"He must have given you a lot of hope", said Jonas.

"He did."

"It must have been nice to feel that." Jonas had a naturally cheerful face, but I saw his smile dim as he said this, as if to admit how little hope he had. "What a mess we've gotten ourselves into." Jonas looked around as he said this. "It must have been nice to live with Connors and his group—to live off of the land, in a natural way. Why didn't you follow them, when they went?" Jonas asked.

"I don't know." I didn't. Jonas looked at me in a sort of perplexed way; then he smiled and chuckled to himself again with a grin that buried the deep scars on his face beneath his wrinkles. Jonas' teeth were crooked and yellowed, and his breath smelled like the smoke of an engine. I imagined how I must have looked to him at that moment. I thought to myself how little personal hygiene I had been practicing recently. At one time, I would have looked down on Jonas, felt pity for him; but it was he who was looking down on me now. I didn't mind it too much, though; it felt good to talk to someone.

I tried to reciprocate and be a good conversa-tionalist with Jonas as well, and I asked him a few questions about where he was from and how he got to where he was. On the other hand, he must have been able to tell that I wasn't very skilled at the art of conversation. I was at least out of practice. Jonas told me some things about where he was from; he talked about his mother and his upbringing. I felt embarrassed as we compared stories. My story was one of loss and defeat. As I reflected back on my life, it seemed like I hadn't had many lucky turns in my past. Jonas' story, from what he told me wasn't as bad. I felt ashamed to have been so defeated so many times. I've always thought that it's worse in life to lose high social status than to just be born into low social status. By this point in my life, I should have had something better for myself, I thought; I should have been somewhere else. Jonas was born into difficult circumstances, and although this life was taking its toll on him quickly, he had grown up in it, and was more used to it.

As we talked, there were some things that Jonas' wasn't comfortable telling me about. I could tell because he seemed reluctant to answer some of my questions, and I certainly didn't want to force him to tell me anything.

At some point, it was time to sleep. I could feel that, as our conversation came to an end, we both felt a certain lack of comfort, and I left Jonas to go find a place to rest. I was almost prepared to ask Jonas for a suggestion on where to sleep, but, for some reason, I didn't. Jonas had his own reasons for not offering me the option of staying where he slept.

Instead I walked away and moved into a maze of alleyways not too far away. I was hoping to find an uninhabited niche; I didn't need much—just a corner somewhere in the dark to lay down for the night. But like my search for food, my search for shelter became much more difficult than I anticipated. Once again, I began having the feeling that the shadows were watching and moving around me as I passed from street to street. I had begun to think that I was going crazy some time around this point anyway, so I uneasily dismissed my feelings as paranoia. After all, I had been through a lot; and even the most stable of individuals has their breaking point. Even though I had just had my first conversation in weeks, and, perhaps, made a friend, I realized how much of a disaster my life was at this point. I had fallen so far from what I once was.

I should have been more focused on survival at this point rather than self-pity, but I was lost in these thoughts when one of the shadows of the alley moved quickly at me—too quickly for me to react. I felt a blunt object hit the side of my head. Vaguely, I caught more shadows coming alive. I was halfway paralyzed and I could feel an electrical tingling throughout my body. Whatever I had been hit with had dulled my mind as well—rendering me stupefied as I fell to the ground. I heard vague laughter overlaying the sound of slurred voices through the electrical buzz ringing in my ears. For a moment, it seemed like the people around me were like the insects that attacked me in the wilderness, and the buzzing of their activity through my paralyzed senses was like the sound of the insects that stung me whenever I was trying to sleep.

Then, the shadows crouched around me and searched my pockets and my satchel for the few remaining possessions that I had. Each time a hand brushed over me, it produced an amazingly painful sense of pins and needles as I tried to react. Even my screams produced no noise as I gasped in a vain attempt to yell. In frustration, one of the figures kicked my stomach realizing that I didn't have anything worthwhile. The others quickly joined in. Each jab of their feet produced a deep, cutting shock that radiated straight through my abdomen. Finally one figure sat on top of me and began pummeling me with his fists. I could make out the words "street vermin" and "food for bugs" in his angered utterances. Whatever weapon I had been stunned by paralyzed my muscles, but heightened my sense of touch, which gave each sensation of contact on my body a bitter, electrical jolt. The ground was hard and each rock in the pavement jutted into my skin like a razor. Most of what I heard was partially drowned out by the low electrical-sounding buzz in my ears. The figures began to remit, as they apparently grew tired or bored of beating me. They crouched beside me and searched through the remainder of my possessions more thoroughly. I could make out their laughter, which sounded distant. Finally, finding nothing of any real value, they decided to simply take everything I had and split it all up elsewhere.

I lay in the dark for at least several hours. At first, I was squirming like a tied-up prisoner, but eventually, I grew tired and accepted my condition. For a moment, I think I even was asleep for a few minutes. When I wasn't moving, being numb gave me some relief from the insects that were now gath-

ering around me. The feeling came back slowly; I
began to feel the warmth of the blood that was
dripping from my mouth. My fingers started moving—then my arms. Finally, I began to recover
enough movement and sensation to brush the insects off of the breaks of my skin into which they
were climbing. As my sense of smell came back I
realized how much I was in need of a bath, or at
least, some clean, running water.

As I stood up, I took off my pants and peeled off
my underwear. As I tried to redress myself, some
figures walked past me and briefly glared at me
with hollow stares. I don't know if their look was
pity or fear. As they passed, part of me wished they
did fear me. I saw their faces as all my antagonists
in this withering civilization. To invoke fear would
have given me at least a modicum of power over
them; but I had no power, and I partly moved my
aching legs enough to walk away.

That moment was probably when I most wished
I could stop existing. And I strongly considered
taking my life somehow, although I didn't have the
means or the energy. I tried again to shake off these
suicidal urges. That night was difficult for me. I
was already exhausted and I was without any kind
of shelter. I knew wherever I slept, the insects
would continue taking bits of my body and my energy.

After that night, things actually got a little better. I fell into a daily pattern, and I got a little better
at panhandling for food with Jonas. Each day, I
earned just enough scraps of food to get me to the
next day. I also more closely aligned myself with
Jonas; he seemed amicable and was a source of
some protection. The day after my attack, I told him

what had happened, he said little and his reaction gave me the impression that this was a common occurrence.

"Yeah, that happens sometimes," he said as he inspected me with pity, looking over my injuries. "I'm sorry. I didn't think they would get to you so soon."

"They got to me," I replied.

"Listen, I'm sorry I didn't offer help sooner, but I was afraid of how forward that might seem. I know how you must feel, though. I used to have to live like that, for a while. I found a place to go here in the city. It's usually sort of safe. Why don't I take you there, if we get some food? At least you'll have a place to sleep." Jonas' brows furrowed as the lines in his face deepened to show his concern, as he looked me over.

The idea of a place to sleep was, I thought, very appealing. "It's safe?"

"Nothing's completely safe."

"I have nothing to give you in return." I looked down and felt ashamed.

"It's okay. You'll pay me back some day." Jonas smiled at me, and I marveled at how kind he was being.

At the end of that day, Jonas took me to the top of an abandoned building. The building was seven stories tall, so the walk up the stairwell wore me out. But when we reached the roof, the view of Newark was truly amazing. I couldn't see the forest that I came from, the smog still blurred the horizon; but I thought I could see most of the city. The gray, tainted buildings stood all around us, and below us we could see the streets and a hundred dark figures milling about. I pointed out along the direction from which I came to Newark. "That's where I first came into the city."

"Where?" Jonas asked.

"Further in that direction," I said. A few miles out that way, there's a wooded area."

Jonas smiled. "You lived over there?"

"Yeah."

"And there's lots of trees over there…?"

"Yeah," I said.

"What about when you were staying with Connors. How did the trees look, do they all bunch together like a forest or what?"

"Sometimes," I replied.

"I don't think I've ever walked around like that among trees. It sounds like a dream-world."

"Connors had a daughter, Patricia. She once told me that, back in the northwest, there are miles and miles of trees and forests."

"Ha!" Jonas laughed at this as though it was ridiculous, but his eyes glimmered with happiness in an excitement that there was a place where the trees grow freely. To Jonas, a place where trees outnumber people was a dream.

He asked me again, "That's where they were going? To the northwest?"

"Yeah."

"Why didn't you go with them?"

"I don't know." I didn't, I had felt a little traumatized by everything that had happened to me since I left Chesapeake City. I guess that, since then, I've had a foreshortened sense of the future. It's been hard for me to plan in anticipation of my next day, since I didn't really believe it would come. After I was exiled from Chesapeake City, I realized how drastically and abruptly my world could change. Now, I seemed to view the future as something that can't be planned for. That may have been part of the reason why I didn't go with Connors and his band.

After our conversation, we both went to sleep. Jonas was kind to me, I thought to myself. I didn't at the time know why. I was tired and I just wanted to sleep.

Chapter VI

The next few days I spent outside of the market store, jostling with the others for a handful of morsels, but I was smart enough at least to know that this lifestyle would not sustain me forever. I learned something else, as I watched the van of men selling "concentrate" come and go. They were cleaner and better fed than most of the crowd—or even the people who worked at the store. Somewhere there had to be food that these people had access to.

After a week of standing outside the grocery store, I decided to follow the truck that the men selling "concentrate" drove. I didn't run after them, but I did watch each turn they made as they drove away. Every day, I followed the truck further away knowing in advance the path it had taken the previous day. Eventually, I had to start leaving earlier so I could catch-up to the point where I had last seen them. Jonas never went with me; he thought my quest to find their "secret hideout" was silly. I admit it must have seemed silly, but I was desperate for more food. I could feel my body weakening; my hair was falling out; my skin was thin and brittle, and my stomach had a constant aching in it. If I could have had one last hearty meal, it would have sustained me for weeks, maybe even months. I thought that the van I was following must have come from somewhere where food was more abundant.

My spirit was getting weaker and weaker throughout this time, and I had to try hard not to resent the people who worked in the grocery store, or the men who were selling concentrate. I've never had a scrupulous sense of morality, but I was slowly giving up whatever ethics I had in exchange for the survival instinct that I needed to exist in this civilization.

One day, I had gotten especially little food. I was too weak to follow the van to where I had tracked it, so I gave up and went back home. As I walked past the grocery store, just during dusk, I saw an old woman huddled in the corner; she was apparently eating some food when she noticed a beetle by one of her feet. I was shocked when she leaned forward to give the beast some bread.

"What are you doing!" I shouted.

She didn't answer—just stood looking at me in fear. Looking back, I should have known she was either insane or demented, by the way she looked confused by everything I said.

"What are you doing!" I grabbed the arm that she was holding her bread in as she winced in pain. I was shocked by my own anger, but I didn't stop long enough to contemplate what I was doing. My mouth watered, as I smelled the food in her hand, even though it was just a piece of bread. She started tearing and was trying to verbalize words to stop me, but it was too late. My hunger coupled with my anger to unleash my instinctive behavior. I grabbed the bread from her and started nibbling on it immediately as I paced away. She caught up with me as I was turning away and grabbed my elbow with her frail hand. Still blinded by rage, I swung my, hitting her face with my fist. I could feel her thin jaw breaking on the other side of my knuckles. As she fell to the ground, I stood over her gobbling the last of her food; it gave me enough of a moment to look down and see her blue eyes, now reddened with tears. My body filled with shame over what I had done. I started sweating and ran away. I ran the entire way back to the building that Jonas was at. As I reached the roof, I collapsed, being overcome somewhere between exhaustion and shame. I now knew the extent to which I was becoming an inhabitant of this new culture.

Seeing me distraught, Jonas approached me and asked what happened. "I'm sorry I'd rather not say," was the only answer I could produce. I was out of breath, and it would have been difficult to talk about what I was feeling anyway. Jonas pushed for more, though.

"It's okay, you can tell me... I want to help you... What happened...? Did you get attacked?"

"No, Jonas. I'm sorry; I don't want to talk about it."

Jonas tried to be compassionate and supportive, but he only made me less comfortable. Finally, I convinced him that I wouldn't discuss what happened at the time, but that we could talk about it later. I knew that Jonas was only trying to be loyal and convince me that he would be a supportive friend, but I was too uncomfortable and ashamed of what had just happened to confide in him.

That night and the next day, I thought about the person I was becoming. It was taking me a long time to learn the lessons that Newark was driving home each day with brutal force. Slowly I was learning that, in this world of scarce resources, every other human was to be considered an enemy. Except for Jonas, almost everyone I interacted with tried to take something from me. I was now returning the brutality that I was taught every time I was attacked. The half-human inhabitants of the city quickly got the better of me, and it seemed that every gain I made in material comfort was counterbalanced by the continued aggressions of my fellow humans against me. Now I was in the crossfire of the battle between two species: the urban human population, and the insect population.

As time passed, my regret over not joining Connor and the others in their travels turned into envy. I resisted the temptation to hate Connors for being smarter than I, and wanting to move further from the old and new cities. Now I thought he might be right. Viewing the broken remnants of humanity around me, I grew more certain of this conclusion.

What was worse than my growing envy of Connor and the others was my gradual blending into this civilization. I'd like to say that I was always the one wronged in Newark by the inhabitants, and that I never stooped to their level of treachery. I'd like to say that I was only the victim, and that I never committed the crimes. While I was in Chesapeake City, I was always comfortable in the knowledge that I was, at least not a malicious person, even if I wasn't a good scientist towards the end of my life there. But the more time I spent in Newark, the more I became like everyone else—clawing and pushing away others for a morsel of food. Every time I caught my reflection, my face looked more gray and my skin more thin and ashen. Similarly, my conscience interfered less and less with the decisions I made.

I found it hard to sleep the next night, despite my exhaustion. When I did fall asleep, I dreamt that I was standing in the alleyway—the same alley where I had encountered the old woman just a few hours earlier. In my dream I was walking toward a crouched figure dressed in the same clothing as the old woman and holding the same food she was holding. When the figure turned toward me, I saw the face of Mark Adler, my employer from Chesapeake City. He was looking at me with the same frightened countenance as she did. Just like in the incident, I tried to snatch his food. When he resisted, I swung my fist at his face. This time, though, I kept punching. His face cracked like an eggshell beneath my blows. Punch by punch, it seemed to disintegrate as it fell to pieces. As his head crumbled, I saw the face of Belinda beneath his face, but in the dream I couldn't control my rage, and I kept punching. Her face then began to crack and disintegrate revealing beneath it the face of Troy, then Patricia, then Leonard, and then Connors. Finally, still beating, the last face was revealed—the face of the old woman.

Instead of cracking and falling apart, she was bleeding as I punched. I felt my knuckles become wet with her blood. I tried more forcefully to stop punching, but blow-by-blow, her blood became thick and gelatinous, holding my arms. It spread up my arms until I couldn't move. Then, it spread to my trunk and down my legs, holding me in place.

Finally, when I was completely stuck, the old woman raised her bread, which now looked much larger, and she stabbed her bread at my face into my mouth. Choking on the crumbs, and trying to resist her, I couldn't breath, and I could feel myself drowning as though I was underwater. The old woman opened her mouth as if to yell at me, but let out a fierce, buzzing hiss instead. The hiss became louder and louder as I choked, and the tarry blood, which now covered my body, came to life. It stung and burned at my skin and shook me.

I awoke to see Jonas standing over me shaking me and swatting at me. The old woman's hiss became the buzz of a hundred large mosquitoes, which were now swarming all around me. Jonas was holding down my arms as he swatted away the insects. Looking back, Jonas must have thought that I was crazy or comatose. Though I was tugging apart the papers I used as a blanket while I was asleep, I was motionless when I awoke—paralyzed by my own guilt, and I remembered looking up at Jonas.

"Hey! Wake up! Wake up!" Jonas kept screaming long after I had awoken. "Wake up!"

"I know," I said finally. "Don't worry. I'm awake."

"What the Hell's the matter with you?" Jonas sounded uncharacteristically angry. "Get up! Stand up!" Jonas was still swatting insects off of me.

Loathsomely, I stood. "I'm sorry, Jonas," I said weakly. I started brushing the insects off of myself.

"That's okay," Jonas said. "But what's wrong, I've never seen anyone sleep through an attack like that"

"Earlier tonight—before I came home, I ran into an old woman in an alley-way. She must have been senile, because she was feeding some bread that she had to this cockroach. She must have thought it was an animal or something. Anyway, I was so hungry... I wanted her food so much... I hit her and ran off. I didn't want to talk about it when I got home because I was kind of ashamed. I guess I was just dreaming about it."

"Listen," Jonas' tone became sympathetic once again. "I know you haven't been here long. It's hard to adjust. Sometimes, I take it for granted that it's easy for me to make choices when it comes to survival. Come with me." Jonas beckoned me to the side of the roof and looked down at the people below. "Look at that man down there."

I looked.

"He's covered in rags," Jonas continued. "He won't last until the morning without being beaten up or taken for all he's worth, which probably isn't much, anyway. Someone tonight is going to mug him, take everything he has, and leave him either dead or close to it. Someone will. Then, the next day, maybe some fortunate soul will toss him a piece of food or bread, and he'll probably only get a few bites before someone else takes it from him. He's just a waste of flesh—walking around, taking up space. So what's the harm in his pain?"

"So you're saying I shouldn't feel guilty if I'm that someone."

"I'm saying somebody has to be." Jonas' tone was warm and consoling which seemed to contradict the message he conveyed to me.

"I guess I feel a little better, then." I didn't feel any better, but I didn't want to. I still wanted to feel guilty. It was, after all, my guilt that separated me from the muggers who victimized me just a matter of days previously. I knew I shouldn't tell Jonas this, though. My guilt separated me from him, as well. Although I still didn't think Jonas was evil or malicious for having this point of view, I felt as though having guilt over what I had done placed me on a higher moral plateau, and I didn't want to imply that to Jonas since he had been my benefactor since I arrived in Newark.

"How did you wake up and hear me so easily?" I asked.

Jonas smiled. "I'm a light sleeper I guess. You don't last long if you sleep too soundly."

We stood on the roof in silence for a few moments.

"Jonas, do you have any family?"

"My mother, I told you about her. We used to be very close, but we grew apart, I guess after a while I was just an expense to her, and after all, I couldn't do much to support her. She eventually married some guy after my father. After that, we grew even further apart." He paused. "Do you?"

"Well, I had Belinda. I told you about her. We never really got around to having a family. Other than that, my mother raised me. I was an only-child also."

"You know, you can still have a family some day."

"In all this?" I asked.

"Not everyone lives like this. There's still people out there who live in houses and complexes with a lot of security. There's still people who can afford to buy their food. Maybe something will come my way someday. Money... a job..."

"Is that what keeps you going?"

"Yeah, I guess."

"I don't know how you keep your motivation, honestly." Jonas must have sensed my frustration and growing apathy as I said this. Jonas smiled sympathetically. "I've only been here a while, and I'm getting so tired of struggling so much for so little." I thought after I said this, that it must have offended Jonas. I was grateful for everything he had given me, but I still thought little of my condition. After that, not much else was said.

Jonas stayed awake for a while longer, sitting on the ledge of the building, but I went back to sleep shortly afterwards. Reluctantly, I was comforted by Jonas' words. I didn't know whether or not I would survive, but in the long run it wouldn't really matter. Humanity didn't have much longer either. In part, my apathy was fueled by the fact that to me, the humans around me were becoming like the insects that I was struggling against every day. Both were chipping away at my life and will power in a piece-meal fashion. If it hadn't been for Jonas I wouldn't have had any chance of survival in Newark, but I knew now that even he had motivations for his kindness.

Jonas Morris was born in Newark, and lived almost all of his life in the city. His mother, Julia gave birth to him when she was only fifteen. She was poor, and his father wasn't even present at his birth. Luckily, Julia had a supportive mother who helped her deliver and raise her baby. Both mother and grandmother were very protective of the new child. Neither though, had a very stable life, and so Jonas' upbringing was under circumstances of extreme poverty. Although he wasn't fully aware of how poor he was, Jonas often went for months at a time without a place to sleep.

Though she loved him very much, Jonas didn't have a chance to get to know his grandmother very well. She died when he was two years old. An older woman, she was chronically ill and had a number of smoldering medical conditions, which were never properly treated. One night, while in bed, she was bitten by a spider on her back. Although a similar wound would have been survivable for most people, hers became infected and necrotic. She died in septic shock. Julia tried to care for her mother as she worsened over the course of only a couple of days, but she deteriorated quickly. When they finally decided that she should be taken to the hospital, it was already too late. Julia was left with a child to care for before she was even eighteen years old.

Julia was eligible for a government program, which allowed her to enroll her child in a kindergarten program. Jonas did well in school, and because of his high marks, he was able to keep going to school for several years. Julia, in the meantime, was a devoted mother and got a job in order to attempt to provide for her son. She began working with a municipal authority in charge of sewage and sanitation. Though it was hard work, Julia was young and was hopeful that the money she earned would help her son.

In elementary school, Jonas continued to do well. He passed his classes easily, and his mother was proud of him. Socially, though Jonas wasn't making many friends at school. As he grew older, he seemed to spend less and less time with children his own age. By the time he was eleven, even his mother sensed there was something different about him.

While other young men were developing their independence, Jonas still seemed to cling to his mother. On the other hand, Julia had to spend more time at work to try to provide more stability for Jonas. When she did come home, Jonas was very demanding and monopolized her time. Over the years, and unintentionally, Julia began to resent Jonas for all the sacrifices she made for him. She felt that she had given her youth to him, and he didn't seem grateful to her. At times, Jonas felt the distance growing between him and his mother.

When she was twenty-eight Julia met an older man at work. Jim Oliver was addicted to a barbiturate intoxicant called lysazine and introduced it to Julia also. Although it didn't seem right at the time, she liked how much the drug made her forget the difficulty of her job. She was also becoming very attached to this new man. He began to spend the night with Julia, and when he finally met her son, he instantly spurned him. He could tell immediately that Jonas was different than other boys, and he also felt how close Jonas was with his mother, even though Julia was feeling increasingly burdened by him now. Oliver was jealous of this closeness, and he saw Jonas as a threat to his relationship with Julia. Before long, when Oliver had a problem paying his rent, it seemed natural that he should move in with Julia. Although she knew the two wouldn't get along, Julia didn't want to give up her new relationship, and she rationalized that Jonas would benefit from having a strong male influence. After Oliver moved in, she gave him more control of their home. At first Jim only verbalized his feelings about Jonas, but as his dislike for Jonas grew, he began to beat him in fits of anger. At first, this only happened while Julia was away, but as time went on, she objected less and less to the way he treated Jonas. She had already given up much in her life for her son, and now, she didn't want to give up her happiness with Oliver. In other ways, Julia now prioritized her new addiction, and there was less money left over for Jonas as time went on. In moments of more intense craving, Julia cursed her son who had always been a heavy financial burden was now an obstacle for her ability to feed her addiction.

Jonas, for obvious reasons started spending time outside his home, but, since he had few friends, and he knew the city was dangerous, he had nowhere really to go. Soon after he turned fourteen, Jonas met Sean, an older boy, who liked spending time with Jonas. Sean was eighteen, and after they met, he helped Jonas make sense of why he felt so different. Sean had similar problems relating to others, especially his family, whom he was never completely honest with. Moreover, Sean helped Jonas get away from his home. By this point Jonas was always visibly bruised or injured by Oliver's beatings. One day, while the two of them were together, Sean's father came home from work unexpectedly.

"Dad!" Sean exclaimed, pushing Jonas away from him.

Sean's father, who had never seen Jonas before, was consumed with rage at the boy who he saw corrupting his son. "Who are you?! Who are you?! What are you doing with my son?!" He picked up Jonas by the back of his neck and flung him face first into a wall, breaking Jonas' nose.

"Dad, stop!" Sean pleaded as his father picked up a baseball bat. But his father looked at him and gave him a cold, hard stare. Sean looked down with shame and sat down on his bed. He stared straight at the ground as he tried to ignore what was going on around him.

In the meantime, Sean's father had thrown Jonas down on the floor, and was kicking him and swinging at his torso and head with the bat. "Please stop…" Jonas said weakly, "Sean…" Sean's father was even more enraged to hear Jonas utter his son's name in such a pathetic voice. After a few more blows, Jonas tried crawling towards the door of the apartment in a vain attempt to escape.

"Please stop," Jonas said again. As he reached the door of the apartment, still crawling, Sean's father planted his boot on the back of Jonas' neck, and the blunt end of the bat against Jonas' head.

"If you ever come back," he said, "you'll beg louder than that." Sean's father opened the door against Jonas' head and pushed the young boy out, and away from his property. "I'll kill you if I ever see you again," he yelled as Jonas staggered away.

Reluctantly, Jonas returned home. He saw Sean again a few days later, but he seemed distant and curt. When Jonas returned home, he looked more badly beaten that he had ever looked after one of Oliver's beatings. His mother saw him, but she didn't want to ask him what happened, fearing that it was her lover who had inflicted Jonas' new injuries. In turn, Jonas, out of shame, didn't want to tell his mother what happened, and risk losing what little love she had left for him. Later that night, she and Jim fought over what had happened to Jonas. Oliver asserted his innocence with little credibility. Ironically, this was the only instance when Julia confronted Jim, but it was the only time that he was innocent. He stared at her with an annoyed look, and she quickly dropped the subject.

Jonas' life at home worsened. He now realized how little his mother cared for his well being, and he was still trying to wrestle with his horrible home life and his personal identity struggle. He wanted to leave, but he had never held a job, and his education was incomplete. Additionally, the world around him was growing worse by the year, and there would be little room for him in the work force even if he could complete his education.

With fewer options at home, Jonas started spending more time on the streets, dangerous as they were. With time, Jonas forgot about Sean, though he thought for a time, that he never would. He met someone else. This time, Jonas met Eric, who was much older, at thirty-six. Eric had his own apartment and took Jonas in while he was between his old home with his mother and Jim Oliver and the streets. Jonas felt comforted, for a while and was happy to live at a subsistence level while he was free from the beatings of Jim Oliver. Jonas' mother was concerned for a time, but Oliver reassured her, and her addiction had deepened to the point that she had little concern left for Jonas.

Jonas was fifteen when he moved in with Eric; he tried to work odd jobs to help out with the rent and bills, but Eric was largely self-sufficient poor as he was. When Jonas was eighteen, though, Eric was killed while coming home from work. Jonas was devastated as well as financially unable to take care of himself. He tried unsuccessfully to look for his mother, but she had, by that time, lost her job and moved several times. He never knew how much her life worsened, but on some level, Jonas felt guilty, as though he had abandoned her. Now that he was older, he realized how much she provided for and supported him throughout most of his youth.

As he sunk even further down, Jonas went back to the streets—this time as a permanent, full-time home. Jonas turned to panhandling for meager scraps of food. He was tall and naturally agile, and as he lived on the streets, he began to learn to defend himself. He lived under these circumstances for several years, before he found his new place to stay, on top of one of the buildings of downtown Newark. Though he wasn't naturally well equipped to live on the streets, he was now much more skilled and knowledgeable about surviving in the city than I was.

The next day, I awoke after Jonas. Jonas was collecting some pieces of a shiny metal instrument and box. It looked like the one that I had been paralyzed with when I first came to Newark.

"What's that?"

"It's like a stun gun, but it's stronger," Jonas replied.

"I didn't know you had one of those."

"I didn't until yesterday. I'd let you keep it, but I plan on trading it for concentrate."

"I didn't know you took concentrate, too."

"Everybody does. Concentrate is like nutrition; it's just food. Do you ever see people in the street with swollen arms and legs and doughy skin?"

"Yeah."

"Those are people who go long enough without concentrate. The scraps we get aren't enough to stay alive on."

"What about me? I'm okay, and I've never taken concentrate." I was still angry over getting beaten up by the men who were selling concentrate; so I didn't want to accept the notion that they were providing something useful.

"Yeah," Jonas replied. "But if you go for long enough without concentrate, you'll get malnourished too. Don't worry, we'll figure out something."

Jonas and I went back to the area of the grocery store. I was still affected by what had happened the previous night, and I looked at the people around me differently; I didn't have as much pity for those around me who were weak or frail. Even though I felt guilty about what I did to the old woman, I remembered how good it felt to eat, and I saw the weaker individuals as objects I might to exploit for food. I tried to resist these thoughts, but I was hungry and hopeless, and I had scarcely enough will power to wake up in the mornings, much less control these powerful impulses.

Early on in the day, Jonas traded the device he had for concentrate. He collected a few containers worth, and went somewhere to take some of it. The rest of it he must have taken back to the rooftop to hide. I went back into the crowd that was jostling for food. I didn't snatch up much for myself, just a couple of morsels, as usual. Jonas returned, as well. He seemed a little giddy, but otherwise, his behavior wasn't out of the ordinary. I thought he probably just felt better to get some nourishment.

When the crowd began to dwindle, I set off to follow the men selling concentrate as I had done many times before. Since I knew in advance the turns they would make. I walked to where I had previously followed them, hoping that I could see their next move. I reached an area a few blocks to a mile away from the grocery store, which was where I lost track of the van the last time that I tried to follow them. Just as I had suspected, the van was following its usual path. Just when it passed me, though, the van abruptly came to a halt, screeching its tires. I knew what this meant. Quickly, two of the men jumped out of the van and ran towards me. I was already running before their feet hit the pavement.

I should have anticipated this happening, I thought to myself. I should have been more careful. This was stupid of me. But there wasn't time to think. I wasn't too familiar with these streets, but I knew I would have better luck in the alleyways. If I kept making abrupt turns, then the men wouldn't be able to keep up with me, and I'd eventually lose them. The risk was running into a dead end.

First, I saw a fence on my right; so I jumped over it, then, over the next fence into the alley on the other side. I didn't look back, but I could hear their footsteps and heavy gasps behind me. I jumped another fence and turned left. I was headed back to the grocery store area. I thought if I could get back to what was left of the crowd, that I would find some safety. I took a fast right around another building, but I could hear that the men were just behind me. I darted around the building and came to a dead end, with a fence. I thought of jumping it; I almost did, but I hesitated for a moment—just a moment, but enough to narrow the gap between the men behind me and myself. I jumped and reached for the top of the fence, when I heard a click from behind me. The men's footsteps stopped. A thin wire whipped against my legs stinging my skin, and paralyzing me from the waist down. Stunned, I lost my grip, slid down the fence face-first, and hit the pavement.

"Get back here, friend." The voice behind me said. I felt a tug on my legs and my body dragged along the pavement back to the men. One of them kicked me over so I was on my back. I started swinging in vain at their legs. It was a foolish effort, but my only option.

"Where are your friends, now, friend?" said one of the men. The emphasis he placed on the word "friend" sounded peculiar to me. Was this word somehow significant? Was it a reference to some organization? I didn't have time to ponder these questions. The van pulled up behind me, and the men went to work on me with the sleek steel rods that they used to threaten me during our last encounter. The third man stepped out of the van, now and watched as they beat me up. I was still on the ground.

"That's enough. Let me have a word with our friend," the third man said. The other two then stopped beating me, but each of them stepped on one of my arms with their boots holding me down. The third man stepped heavily on my face with his boot pushing my head against the pavement. "Listen, friend. I don't know what you're planning, and I don't care. We're not afraid of you. If it were up to me, I would kill you right now. I don't need this city to be crawling with friends. But if you ever try something this stupid again, I will kill you."

One of the other men came around to my head and started kicking my face, while the third man's boots held it in place. I struggled, though, and quickly, the third man lost his grip on my head enough to stop. Instead, the two other men turned me over and held me down with my face against the pavement. The third man took out a thin strand of metal and began whipping it against my back. I could feel my skin tearing and coming up off of my back. All along, I was screaming out. "I'm not a friend. I don't know what you're talking about." But that didn't make any difference. The third man continued to whip me until I was begging for him to stop. The men were all laughing throughout.

Finally, the man stopped whipping me. He kneeled on my back and pushed against my head. "Now, you go tell all your friends about this, and make sure and get them all riled up, okay." With this the men laughed and walked back to the van.

Though I was weak, I knew I would be food for bugs if I didn't quickly get up. The feeling quickly returned to my legs.

When I left the alley, there was a woman standing just outside it, standing as though she was waiting for me. "Are you a friend?" she asked. Considering the beating I had just endured, I was profoundly irritated by this question, and I made my irritation obvious to her, by the expression on my face.

"No. I'm not a friend," I replied. I looked into her eyes; they were deep and dark. She looked young, and somehow familiar to me. "Do I even know you?"

"I've seen you before, in the crowd by the grocery store," she said. "And I was there, when you challenged the men. It's okay, I'm a friend." The way she used the word "friend" again implied that there was more to this word than the meaning I understood.

"You obviously, didn't see what just happened."

"No," she said. "I saw everything."

"You saw everything that just happened?" I asked in astonishment.

"Yes," she said, "that's why I wanted to talk to you."

"You waited here to talk to me? They could have killed me!" I was being rather terse and rude, but I thought, that if this woman was a "friend", then I should probably stay away from her, given what had just happened to me.

"I'm sorry," she said.

"No problem. Thanks for the help, friend." I said the word "friend" with sarcastic emphasis; with this I walked off as quickly as I could, my arms and legs still sore. I don't know what I did to upset the men in the van so much, but I gathered that they thought I was somehow associated with this young woman.

By the time I made it back to the rooftop that I had been staying at, Jonas was already there. I reached the roof and found him shaking an old man. "Who told you to come up here? Who told you to come up here?" Jonas' voice was filled with anger; he was standing holding the old man dangerously close to the edge of the roof.

"Jonas!" I shouted.

He glanced over at me, and instantly recognized that I had just been beaten. Blood was still dripping out of my nostrils and mouth, and my eyes were beginning to swell to the point that they were nearly shut. As soon as Jonas turned some of his attention toward me, though, the old man began squirming to try to get away. Jonas pushed him against the ledge and swung at his face.

"Jonas, he's going to fall! Stop it!" But before I could reach Jonas, he had delivered a final blow, which sent the old man over the ledge and down to his doom. He shrieked as he fell in a weak, raspy voice. "My god, you killed him, Jonas, you killed him."

Jonas saw that I was profoundly disturbed. "I had to, he was trying to find food up here." I stared at Jonas while he said this, shocked, and obviously not pacified by his explanation. "He was snooping around," Jonas continued. "He would have come back."

"No. You didn't have to kill him."

Jonas' tone became more soothing and soft as I became more angered. "Listen, I'm sorry you saw that, it'll be okay."

"Jonas, you just killed a helpless old man." In addition to feeling so much physical pain, I was beginning to feel nauseated. I stood over the ledge looking down at the motionless body with its limbs contorted. Then, after a moment, I turned to walk away.

"Where are you going?" Jonas asked with almost a mirthful tone.

"I have to go," I said.

As I left, Jonas was pleading with me. "Enough!" I exclaimed. "If I had gotten here sooner, I would have stopped you."

By the time I reached the stairwell, Jonas' tone became angered. "You'll never survive like that! Would you rather let any vagrant up here? You'll never even survive on your own! It's okay for you to beat up an old lady, but I can't defend my territory, eh?" He was right, there. I turned around and looked at him. I had no retort. As I looked into his eyes, and saw how apathetic he was regarding what he had just done, I saw my future. Would I become a killer? Maybe. Probably, if I stayed here, but I was already gone. I'm not good at a lot of things, but I knew one thing that I could do was walk away from something.

"Wait a second, we can talk this out," Jonas continued. I walked down the stairs, out the bottom floor, and into the street.

I kept walking that night, for hours. It had been a long day. Luckily, no one else mugged me. Maybe they saw how badly beaten I was, and assumed someone else had gotten to me first—that wouldn't be far from the truth. For the most part, I didn't much care what happened to me now anyway. I knew that the longer I stayed in Newark, the more I would become like those around me. I would eventually either lose my morality and adapt to my surroundings, or be killed if I failed to prioritize my survival at the expense of others. Both outcomes seemed equally unappealing. I didn't think I could last long on my own, but I no longer cared if I didn't.

Chapter VII

In retrospect, I was surprised that I became as upset as I was at Jonas. Not only because he had done so much for me, but also because I had never yelled like that at anyone. In fact, I didn't remember ever before standing up to anyone over any issue. I certainly couldn't remember feeling that emotional in my recent past. I thought to myself, the cloud that once surrounded my mind had now completely disappeared, but now I had an entirely different array of problems.

I was once again alone. I probably wouldn't have survived in urban surroundings if it weren't for the help of Jonas, and now I wouldn't last long. A small part of me was relieved. Jonas was kind to me, but he had motivations—reasons for his kindness. I was grateful now to end the intrusions into my sleep, which I was trying to forget.

I tried not to think of the things that Jonas had wanted from me. The human mind has an amazing ability to construct defenses when the psyche is threatened, especially when the only remaining options are as poor as they were for me. I had a number of mental exercises, weak as they were, to try to erase my memories. Then again, there wasn't much for me to escape to in my life. Aside from the feeling of eating, which was a rarity, I had experienced very few pleasant feelings since leaving Connors and his band.

The next day, I was hoping to see again the woman who had followed me and seen me get beaten up the previous night. She was one of very few people who had talked to me while I had been

in Newark, and she was the only female that I had
spoken to at all since Patricia. I'm sure that in
Chesapeake City, I might have considered her plain,
but in Newark, I found her mere femininity to be
very attractive. Part of me wanted to know more
about the "friends" that she spoke of, even though I
had already been beaten up a couple of times because of this mysterious organization that I knew
nothing about. If they were powerful enough that
the men selling concentrate feared them, they must
have been an important organization. I already
shared with the "friends" a common enemy; perhaps I could find more in common with them. There
was a feeling of camaraderie that I felt with Connors and his band that I would have liked to recap-
ture, especially as lonely as I was in Newark.

The next day I hung around the grocery store
where I had seen the woman many times previously.
By the end of the day, I hadn't found her, and I was
again becoming hungry and tired. As I walked to
another area around the grocery store, turning a
corner, I saw, instead, one of the men who were
selling concentrate earlier. I was within a couple of
feet of him when I recognized him. He smiled as he
looked down and recognized me. Physically imposing as he was, the other two men weren't far
away from him. I wasn't a match for him—much
less his two partners—especially since I was nearly
starving. I turned and ran, and this time, I got away.
Looking back, I'm sure they let me go. They didn't
have to fight me again; they knew I was beaten.

That night, I wished they had caught up with
me. My ability to secure sleep and food was once
again lost. I walked the streets for hours searching
for what might be a safe place. While I was walking

by one building, I caught a look at my arms in the glow of the street lamp. They were covered with excoriations, and deep scars. They had become thinned and wasted. The skin of my arms now hung empty from my bones. I was wasting away and taking on the gray color of the other inhabitants of Newark. I only wished now that someone would finally finish me off.

Three days passed, as I got worse and worse. The beatings, hunger, and chronic sleepiness, which were already familiar to me, now became a daily fact. Once again, I was giving up on life, and I had almost mustered up enough courage to actively end my life and solve my problems. With the little strength that I had left, I could still climb a flight of stairs to the top of an abandoned building and throw myself off. It was a liberating feeling to fantasize about my death and the only thing that gave me any positive energy. Freedom from my suffering was a persuasive thought. Thinking about my body plunging to death even gave me a small rush of adrenaline, and maybe gave me just enough energy to continue living. Besides, if I didn't think about suicide, I could only think about my hunger, fear, and pain.

On the fourth day, I again found myself at the grocery store. This time, though, I found the woman who had seen me get beaten up several nights previously. I filled with joy when I saw her, as though I had undertaken a long journey just to find her. She looked especially meek when she saw me, though everyone here seemed to have a similar look of meekness. I realized she might be somewhat frightened by me after what she saw several days earlier. In a way, I was more scared of her.

We exchanged hellos and she must have seen that I wanted to talk to her more than I did at our first encounter.

"You have a great deal of courage," she said.

I thought this odd. "It doesn't take much courage to run away, get caught, and then get beaten up." I must have sounded mean or sarcastic saying this, but as much as I wanted to have more of a conversation with her, I didn't have the energy for courtesy.

"Yes, but you've been following those men for some time."

"They look healthier and cleaner than any of us. I just wanted to see where they came from, and if they had food."

She seemed angered by this. "They are agents of the cities."

"The cities?"

"Yes," she said. I thought at first that this woman must be crazy, but I hadn't seen or talked to anyone, much less a woman in such a long time. Though she wasn't very attractive, the sound of a woman's voice talking to me was very soothing. If I had had more energy at that time, I probably would have been very attracted to her.

She continued. "The cities send them out to peddle concentrate to the masses. It's all a part of their scheme. You must know about these things. I thought that's why you were antagonizing those men."

I thought I should agree with this. "I had a suspicion. How do you know so much of these men and concentrate?"

"My name is Corrina. I am a Friend. We're an organization. We have a leader and an ambition to someday stop the cities and their plans for the rest of the world." Corrina had glassy blue eyes and spoke of her convictions with an almost hypnotized look to her face. Her thin, bony fingers gesticulated urgently and were evidence of the conviction she had in everything she said.

Corrina did most of the talking in our conversation. I was dumbfounded as she spoke so seriously about her cause and its impact on the future of humanity.

The Friends turned out to be a loosely organized movement led by a woman named Ida Petrovich. The organization spanned several of the still populated old cities, mostly in Northeast America and Canada, but apparently some of the contacts of the organization were worldwide. The Friends had uncovered the plans of the new cities to slowly depopulate the rest of the globe. Petrovich theorized that the new cities of the world had a tightly organized and oligarchic central core government, which was both elite and clandestine. She disseminated her conspiracy theories through her own speeches and through the ranks of her followers, who traveled to other cities to recruit new followers.

Corrina and I talked for about two hours. Briefly, I could forget my hunger while I stared at her. I was impressed that such a timid and meek figure would espouse such grand and contentious ideas. However, I was never a political creature. My social skills and articulacy never provided me with an opportunity to be involved in any political arena, and I probably would still want only to keep to myself even if I had the necessary skills to be a politician. But I didn't yet want the conversation to end.

"How is it you know so little about these things?" Corrina asked, "Though we have tried to keep our ranks and our numbers secret, most people have already heard of our organization." Probably by this point in the conversation, Corrina sensed how much of a newcomer I was in Newark, though my appearance now completely blended into that of the population around me.

I debated whether or not I should tell Corrina about my background. With such hostility toward the new cities, Corrina probably would have responded unkindly if she knew that I once lived in Chesapeake City. I decided, though, to tell her. Once again I found myself conveying the same story of my life.

I told Corrina about my exile from Chesapeake City, the time I spent with Connors and his group, and the recent time I had lived with Jonas. The story was beginning to become hackneyed to me. Strange that it moved her so much. Having lived through it, it wasn't so interesting to me. I was more surprised that Corrina didn't seem to mind much that I was from Chesapeake City. I feared she would consider me part of the system she was fighting against. As radical as her beliefs sounded, I was glad she didn't hate me.

Telling her the story of my life took a lot out of me. I told Corrina I was hungry.

"Here, have something to eat," she said. With this she produced from her pocket a small handful of oatmeal grains, which I anxiously chewed and swallowed down. My mouth salivated as I chewed, but it felt strange to even have food in my mouth again.

"You must know very much about the organization of the cities—their security. You've walked through the perimeter, also?"

"Yes."

"The eventual goal that we have is to someday gain control of one of the new cities. Once we can tear down the walls, we can gain access to the technology, the machinery, and the food in the cities." I was horrified that Corrina had such destructive ambitions toward the city. "We aren't just out to destroy the new cities and all the people who live in them," she assured me. "We just want to distribute the wealth and technology to the rest of humanity. What the cities are keeping secret could be the keys to saving everyone in the rest of the world."

Since my exile from Chesapeake City, I at times still clung to the foolish ambition of returning to one of the new cities some day, so the idea of attacking one of the new cities didn't settle well with me. On the other hand, I didn't want to get myself into a political debate on the merits of the existence of the new cities—merits that I knew were few anyway. I was grateful to Corrina for the food she gave me, and I would have agreed to almost anything she said.

"I think we would be very excited if you would help us. You were a scientist in Chesapeake City, yes? You could be very helpful to us."

When I was very young, I remember the idealistic feeling that there should be some cause in my life—that I should have some goal that I could pursue to make myself feel noble and my life seem meaningful. I had long since dismissed these thoughts as childish and dramatic, but the conviction that Corrina had in her cause was emotionally moving. Besides, my options at this point were few if I hoped to continue to survive. I suppose that if I hadn't agreed to help Corrina, my only other choice would have eventually been to leave Newark with what few supplies I still had. At least when I was living in the wilderness outside Newark, I was surviving more easily. I could always chew on some of the edible species of plants and leaves for a small amount of sustenance. There, I had only the insects to contend with for survival. Here in Newark, I was caught in the crossfire between humans and insects, with both sides encroaching upon my survival. Since my options were so limited, I agreed to help Corrina. After everything she told me, I was curious to see more of her organization for myself.

The next day, Corrina arranged for my travel on a jeep that was passing through Newark. The Friends, through their loose organization, still had the ability to arrange for transportation from city to city. Corrina was one of the few members of the Friends in the area of Newark that I was in, she said, but, in some other parts of the city, the Friends were much more plentiful. And apparently, in other cities, the Friends had even greater numbers. Corrina must have been somewhat high-ranking in the loose organization. Most of the others that I met had a vague sense of allegiance to the Friends, and identified themselves with Ida Petrovich, but their communication with the rest of the organization was loose and informal. Few of them could answer questions I had about their organization as Corrina could. Even fewer held all of the same theories that Corrina espoused. But they did all share a common inimicality toward the new cities and the elite population that they blamed for their poor quality of life.

My transportation was arranged from one part of the city to another by the Friends, and finally, to an area out of Newark. For this part of the journey, I was transported on a well-armed truck to Annapolis, the city where Ida Petrovich had constructed the informal headquarters of the Friends. This was geographically close to Delaware City, a newer, more advanced city, and a central governing point in the new order of the elite cities.

The last leg of my trip was made with a member of the Friends named Jonathan Dirgo. Again, there was no clear indication of his rank, but he must have been a higher-ranking member of the Friends since the other members on the truck were deferring to him for leadership. Also on the truck were some supplies: oxygen tanks, facemasks, and fuel. I was carried in the back of the truck as the supplies were. Dirgo was riding in the back with me. Though he was their leader, he seemed shy and nervous around me. I didn't quite know why. I sensed an uncertainty about him. He kept asking questions about living in Chesapeake City, but with a tone dissimilar to that which other Friends had as they spoke with me. Beyond the strategic concerns for the city and potential weaknesses, he also wanted to know what it was like to live there. In answering his questions, I was trying not to glorify my life there. I didn't want to offend or undermine his commitment to the Friends and their movement against the new cities. On the other hand, it was almost impossible to not make my life there sound luxurious. The fact that food was never a question for me there, alone, made the city sound like a paradise to Dirgo. As I told my story, I regretted very much leaving Chesapeake City.

"Where did you live? Tell me how people there live," he asked me.

"Each family, or more accurately, each couple, had small apartment-type units that they lived in. Since the city was organized entirely prior to being built, all the residential areas are close to one another." My voice was cracking as I tried to speak loudly above the rattling engine.

"Not like here, eh? Living like a bunch of rats in a sewer, eh?" he laughed, almost inappropriately as he said this, and, in fact, laughed out of proportion with what he was saying many times during the conversation. I didn't want to say anything to sway his opinion about the new cities either way. "I'll bet that everyone there in Chesapeake lived like pigs. Didn't they? Didn't they?" He nudged me as he said this smiling with a yellow-toothed grin.

"It was a wasteful way to live," I said.

"They all deserve what's coming to them."

"What's coming to them?"

"I don't know, yet," Dirgo said. "But someday, they'll get it."

The conversation went on like this. Dirgo continued to deride the people of the new cities, but he had a subtle respect for me as a former member of that civilization. To him, only his imagination and my hazy recollections could provide a picture of life inside the new cities. He must have imagined it as a sort of heaven that had been bestowed on so many undeserving souls. I thought back and remembered the personalities of the people I knew in Chesapeake City. There, the people were self-assured, and, in a way, happy to look down at the plight of humanity. In another way, though, the people there were weak. They couldn't survive outside the thin walls, which protect their lifestyles from the outside. I was a case-in-point of this.

I thought for a moment of what might happen if the walls of the city were ever to fall. The people I had known since leaving Chesapeake City were meek, and frightened, but they were strong enough to survive on so little food and shelter in a world that no longer favored the survival of a human species. The rich in the new cities were threatened by the thinness of their flimsy walls. The poor in the old cities were threatened by the forces of evolution, which were now marginalizing them out of existence.

I learned later that Dirgo must have been a very high-ranking member of the Friends. Apparently, he regularly had audience with Ida Petrovich, and was considered, by many, to be her right-hand. I had no idea what I would think of the rest of the Friends, at this point, but I was anxious to see Petrovich, after seeing how much her followers revered her. On the way to Annapolis, our vehicle made a few stops to collect more passengers, Dirgo introduced me to a cadre of other high-ranking members of the Friends. Some of them looked at me with eagerness; some with disappointment and perhaps hostility; some hoped I would give them new insight into the weaknesses of the cities; some just wanted to know what it was like to live in Chesapeake City.

I learned more as I listened to Dirgo and the other Friends. The rank and file members of the organization were held together loosely with tenuous allegiance to Petrovich and her ideals. Without her, the Friends probably would have disintegrated or splintered into factions. Petrovich, though, was the only strong figurehead in the organization. No other leaders could challenge her role as the central ideologue for the Friends. Besides, her message was simple: unite against the common enemy—the new order of cities. Her techniques of recruiting so many followers and developing alliances with disenfranchised citizens in the new cities, were the reasons why the Friends had become such a potential threat to the new cities.

We arrived in Annapolis the next day. At several points we drove past large trucks on the side of the road filled with well-armed men. It was difficult to tell if any of these men were part of the roaming gangs I had heard about, or if they were part of Petrovich's organization. Since her organization had no official emblem or insignia, it was difficult to identify those who were Friends. As we passed these men on several occasions, though, it was obvious they had some sort of respect for us that prompted them to leave us alone and let us pass unharmed.

It was refreshing to see even the scant trees and greenery on the sides of the roads on the way to Annapolis, if only because of the stark contrast to the ubiquitous gray hues of the city that I had seen while I was in Newark. But as we neared the city of Annapolis, the greenery disappeared and the surroundings turned to gray once again.

When we arrived in Annapolis, it seemed to me to look very much the same as Newark. The human population was increasingly concentrated toward the center of the city. There were more people lying in the streets, looking hungry and wasted. In contrast with Newark, though, the influence of the Friends in this city was obvious. There was one way to tell the difference between a Friend and an otherwise politically uninvolved member of the population. Most people had a glazed-over, exhausted look in their eyes—as though they had been hypnotized and were merely going through the motions of consciousness. If someone was a Friend, the look in their eyes was more keen, and gave their face a look which lay somewhere between anger and concentration. They looked like they had a mission. Some of them believed they did. I noticed this look on many more faces in Annapolis. Unfortunately, though, there was little other difference between the two populations. Both were obviously ravaged by the combined forces of hunger and urban decay. The association of some of the people with the Friends apparently offered them little protection from being beaten up or mugged or from being stung and slowly eaten alive by the flourishing insect population.

We drove to a high building that otherwise didn't stand out from the rest of the nearby buildings. There were a number of men walking casually around the building carrying weapons and trying to look inconspicuous. Dirgo took me to a room several floors up from the ground. As we passed some of the floors, I thought I smelled something that resembled either food or mold. Dirgo took me to an empty-looking room where another member of the Friends was waiting for me at a table. The two men sat on the other side of the table from me and began to question me in detail about the life in Chesapeake City. Dirgo asked me more detailed questions about the perimeter of the city, specifically the pesticide cloud and the turbines used to keep the pesticides away, carefully taking notes as I spoke. The other man was trying to look intimidating and angry with me. I imagined that if he lived in one of the new cities, he would have looked like a large, impressive man. But here he had difficulty looking threatening. His nose had obviously been dislocated several times; he had boils on his forehead and cheeks; and his skin was covered in pockmarks and scars. He, at first, was trying to ask me questions apparently to question my loyalty, but once he saw that I was answering all their questions as willingly and honestly as I could, his focus turned to questions about the infrastructure of the new cities.

I had no reason to lie or try to conceal any information. By this point I realized I had no realistic hope to return to one of the new cities. I guess by that point, I had become somewhat jaded against the new cities, because of that. The other man was curious about the main power plants that provided energy to the city. As they asked me questions, though, both men seemed dismayed by what I told them. I sympathized with them. They must have been hoping that I would expose some vulnerability that they hadn't yet considered, but I realized, as we spoke, how well designed the cities were from a defensive standpoint.

That evening I was provided a meal in a large room with Dirgo, the other man, and a number of others. Petrovich was apparently unavailable and was secluded somewhere busily working, but I had heard so much about her, that I was anxiously awaiting meeting her. The meal consisted of a moldy paste, which was administered in dirty bowls. The bowls had obviously not been washed, but looked like they were wiped clean. The paste tasted remarkably filling and delicious, probably as a result of my hunger. I tried to resist the temptation to scarf it down too fast. I knew it would be more satisfying if I ate it slowly. There was no opportunity for another bowl, and many were unable to eat due to the limited supply. The room we were in, which occupied almost that entire floor of the building, was packed entirely with Friends. Since there were no tables or chairs, some of us were sitting, but most of us were standing in the corner of the room or against one of the walls.

At one point, when some young men were shuffling past us, I noticed one young man who had recently been beaten up. He had bushy hair and a youthful look in his eyes. After this young man passed me, I realized he looked familiar to me because he was Troy, Patricia's lover, from Connors' band. He was almost hard to recognize because of all the scars on his face. He looked horrible and malnourished, and I imagined how bad he would have thought I looked if I had gotten his attention. None-the-less I was glad to see him. I decided to leave Dirgo's side and look for Troy after I realized who he was. I made an arrangement to meet up with Dirgo later in one corner of the large room later.

After a couple of minutes of weaving through the crowd, I caught up with Troy. He was easy to find, and even though he looked worse than when I had last seen him, he still stood out from the rest of the crowd. "Troy. Troy." I caught his shoulder with my hand as I began to catch up with him.

"I... I remember you," he said. He looked as though he was happy to see me, but his happiness was restrained—buried under a very somber countenance that I had never seen him express before.

"You've become a Friend," I asked. He looked at me strangely as though he had never heard that word before, and then smiled.

"A group of Friends found me. Luckily they took pity on me, and took me in." As he said this, I grasped that he didn't leave Connors band under happy circumstances.

"Connors, Patricia, the others? What happened?"

"They're dead. We were traveling, when some gang blocked off one of the highways. There was nothing we could do to avoid them. Then another truck sideswiped us and we fell over. I guess they figured out that Connors was our leader, so they killed him after they beat the rest of us. I was actually unconscious for most of it. When I came to, everyone else was either dead or unconscious. Connors was dead, and Patricia was gone."

I didn't want to point out to him that Patricia might still be alive. I knew it wouldn't give him any solace if I pointed out what else they might have done to her. By now she was probably dead anyway. Troy looked old and tired. "I'm sorry," was all I could say. I was.

"You look like you've been doing alright," Troy said, probably trying to be nice. I didn't want to overplay the things that had happened to me. None of them were as bad as what Troy had been through. Troy lost people he loved and cared for.

"I'm doing okay. So far the Friends have been good to me."

"Petrovich is right," said Troy. "I'm angry at the men who did that, but our real enemies are in the new cities. They're the ones who have turned us against each other." Troy was young enough to have energy behind his anger, and he still had a spirit. He was looking for an enemy and for a fight. I didn't think then how soon he would find one. When Troy spoke like this, the spark returned momentarily to his eyes. For most of the rest of the conversation, his eyes were glazed over and aged like an old man's. "There's going to be a war coming," Troy continued. "Petrovich is going to lead us in an attack against one of the new cities. I think it's going to happen soon."

Troy and I talked for about an hour. I told Troy that I was glad that the Friends had found him, but after the conversation I was overtaken by guilt. Out of a stupid, unrealistic hope to return to one of the new cities, I was able to cheat the fate that Connors and his band suffered. I didn't feel like I was worthy of being saved—of surviving while the rest of them died, especially when I thought of Connors. He was a great man, and I had thought of him frequently since I left his small community. I felt even guiltier when I realized that, when I first arrived in Newark, I was jealous of Connors and his group.

In another world, Patricia and Troy would have had a happy life and raised a family. That should have been the end to his story. Seeing how much he had aged, I realized how little hope there is in the world for humanity. Troy was once youthful, healthy, and optimistic; seeing his mind, body and spirit so weakened, I realized the world that he and I shared was far more powerful than the tenacity of the human spirit.

When I met up with Dirgo later, he directed me to the quarters where I would sleep that night. They were on another floor of the building with nothing but rows and rows of bunk beds. Dirgo told me to sleep on one of the bottom bunks. As I lay down, I realized that this was the first time that I had slept on a bed since I left Connors and his group. I felt instantly comfortable as I lay down on that padded bed, and the pain that I felt in each bruise, and each insect bite in my skin, began to leave my body. I was just barely able to enjoy this sensation, though, since I fell asleep almost immediately.

When I first saw Petrovich, I was in the rear of a small group looking at her back. It was the next day, and she was standing out on a ledge high in a building in what was once downtown Annapolis. I was one of many in an adjoining room watching her look at an audience below her. First, Dirgo stepped forward to introduce her, addressing the audience below.

"Friends," he started. "Friends, we have the power—the ability now to bring our cause into a new level. The future social order can be molded as we see fit." The audience cheered these statements and Dirgo seemed to glow as they supported his words. "Soon, we will not have to face the tyranny of the elite, isolated in their utopian cities. Many of you have already seen the person I am about to introduce. You have heard her speak, and you know the words she says, because they reverberate with the thoughts we have all had in our hearts at times. If you have not heard her before, consider what she says, and consider what we are offering—a chance at a better life."

Dirgo stepped back from the balcony to make way for Petrovich. The narrow streets were filled in all directions as her voice boomed and echoed through the primitive amplification system and off of the skyscrapers and buildings aligning the streets. Her frame was narrow and aged. Her narrow fingers and hands waved and gesticulated sharply with each point she made, reminding me of the way Corrina spoke.

"Friends, we are gathered here together because we all have a common enemy. Look around you, each of you. Those people next to you are packed so closely to you, and pressed against you, because we have all suffered the same plight. Now, you are here because you believe that you have a common enemy. It isn't the insects in the sky and in the earth, though they have ravaged our world. It isn't the criminals and assailants in our streets; they have turned against each other out of frustration. The real enemy we face is a population that has forgotten that we are a part of the same species. It is the population that leeches off of the land we share, and condemns the rest of us to suffer in hunger and poverty. Yet have we ever seen this enemy? Think to yourselves. Have you ever known or even seen anyone from the new cities." There was a moment of silence in the audience, except for the echoes of some remaining cheers. I felt somewhat embarrassed at this point.

"You may have seen their cities, looming in the horizon under a green haze. But unlike the criminals who attack us in our streets, or the insects, which cover the air and every surface we touch, the rich in the elite cities hide behind their masks, constructed of layers and layers of technology, chemicals, and walls. I once believed that their walls were designed to protect them from the insects and the harshness of the climate—that one day, the walls would spread to encompass the rest of humanity. But consider, now, whom the walls are meant to keep out. Look again at each person around you. You are the enemies of these cities of the future; you are the reasons why the walls are built so high. We are the people that the cities are trying to keep out."

The audience cheered wildly as the tone of her voice climaxed at this point.

"Friends, I had the sadness to witness the tragedy of an infant dying recently. She was born maturely and healthy, and she had been healthy for most of her young life. I placed my arms around this infant as she passed away. She looked at this point, up until she died, still completely healthy to me. Do you know what killed her? Can any of you guess?" Again there was silence in the audience.

"I don't know what disease it was." She paused. "I don't have any idea what disease she succumbed to. But do you think they do in the cities? Do you think that, if she lived in the cities, she would have died a mysterious cause without being attended to even by a doctor? She was born with a curse that she is not a member of the sliver of population that is privileged to live in the new cities. So she gets little food, and no medical care, and dies silently with only the voices of her parents as her consolation. Friends, we don't see the faces of those who live in the cities; we see the faces of our children who suffer and die while the cities shield their technologies from us. What do they give us? They poison us with pesticides. They peddle to us concentrate; and they curse us from atop their high shelter inside the cities." Again the audience cheered as their anger rose up from the streets below under the command of Petrovich's voice.

"Friends, you have been listening to me speak of the tyranny of elitism for too long. You have patiently listened to these sermons while you have gone to sleep hungry night after night, while you have suffered with those around you, and while you have waited for your loved ones to die of diseases which are obsolete in the new cities. Now, let us stop waiting. I have long since realized that there is no crime in draining the life from the cities. They have watched and aided as we have spilled our own blood. There is no crime in tearing down their walls of protection. They shouldn't try to hide from members of their own species. And there is even no crime in killing those people whose lives will only serve to find new ways to watch the rest of us die."

The rage and energy of the audience climaxed with Petrovich's voice as she made these last points. I knew now that there would soon be an offensive planned against one of the cities, both because of Petrovich's words and also because of what I had heard from Dirgo and Troy the previous day.

When Petrovich's speech was finished, she raised her wizened hands above her head to soak up the cheers of the people crowding the streets below her. Dirgo stood next to me after his introduction of Petrovich and told me that she wished to speak with me. Before too long, the audience began to disperse and Petrovich moved back into the small crowd behind her. She moved about the crowd shaking each person's hand and urging them to keep firm their commitment to the Friends. She spoke with Dirgo last, who introduced the two of us.

"Ida Petrovich, I want to introduce this man to you. He has come to us as a former citizen of Chesapeake City and has given us important tactical and strategic information," said Dirgo.

"Thank you for your help." Petrovich looked at me with aged but discerning eyes, and I thought that if I was trying to keep any secrets from her, that she would be able to ferret them out. "Tell me, are your loyalties divided? You have come from a civilization where you would live much better than this." She motioned with her hands to the building and people around her.

"I wouldn't be disloyal," I replied. "I've seen the order of the world that the new cities have brought about, and I have to agree that they are draining the life out of humanity." I was surprised that I was expressing myself so eloquently. I felt the wave of passion and conviction that rushed over the audience as Petrovich spoke a few moments ago.

"Remember," Petrovich said as she pointed at me, "you are among the rest of us now—whether you consider yourself to be or not. You are as much an enemy of the new order of cities as I am. Come with me, I will talk to you more."

Towards the end of this conversation, Dirgo walked off to talk to some of the other people who were gathered in the small crowd. Petrovich took me with her into a small office on another floor. I was amazed at how easily she climbed the stairs; she looked old and frail, but she seemed hardly out of breath after climbing several flights of stairs. When we reached the small, plain room that she used as an office, I was impressed by how empty it was. There was a small desk on one side of the room, and an elaborate set of communication equipment on the other side of the room.

"Tell me. Why did you leave Chesapeake City?"

"I was forced to leave, to be honest." I started by telling Petrovich about my failures at work, and my frequent arguments with Mark Adler. I was surprised to hear that Petrovich knew about Adler. Apparently, he was rapidly rising in the ranks of the new cities. Petrovich stared at me with a piercing stare, which made me feel like a surgical patient under a hot light in an operating room. She listened patiently while I spoke.

"Let me ask you two questions," said Petrovich. "There is an anti-aging regimen available in the new cities. It is a regimen of medications and injections, coupled with sterilization. Were you on this regimen?"

I said yes, with some embarrassment that must have been apparent to Petrovich.

"Were you ever involved in a violent crime in any way?" She asked.

I said no, at first, but upon further reflection, I remembered the incident in the alleyway, during which I was involved in a brief fight. I was surprised that Petrovich was guessing so well about events in my life of which she should have had no knowledge.

"You may be surprised by what I have to tell you. The cities have a very vested interest in preventing violence. Any disorder in one of the new cities is simply intolerable." I nodded in agreement, as Petrovich spoke. "The new cities have advanced understanding of pharmacology at their disposal. So, when someone is involved in a violent crime,

his or her aggressive impulses are controlled phar-
macologically. Guilt or innocence doesn't matter in
this area. So if you were the victim or the assailant
you would be treated the same way. It's simply not
worth the resources in the new cities to determine
and assign guilt. So when someone is involved with
a violent crime, various other agents are mixed in
with their anti-aging regimen."

"So, you believe that Chesapeake City may have
put some sort of drug into my anti-aging regimen to
prevent me from being aggressive?" I asked. This
seemed far-fetched at first.

"Yes. I believe further, that your accidents and
mistakes at work may have been the results of these
medications. You see, these medications have to be
precisely titrated depending on the person receiving
them. When they are not, global depression and loss
of intellectual functioning ensues."

I thought back to the mental cloud that I felt I
was under towards the end of my time in Chesapeake City. I also thought back to the increasing
lucidity that I felt when I was among Connors'
group. Watching me, Petrovich must have seen how
deep in reflection I was with this revelation. "I
thought that for some reason, that I wasn't thinking
clearly towards the end of my time in Chesapeake
City. The doctors there used to tell me that I was
becoming senile, and that my brain wasn't as well
preserved by the anti-aging treatments," I told Petrovich.

"That's not very likely," she replied. "I've seen a
lot of people who have been through similar sce-
narios. The two factors, which remain constant for
each person is that they were receiving the anti-
aging treatments, and that they were involved in a

violent crime." Petrovich paused. "I know this must be a strange moment for you. It's a hard thing to realize that you were being unwittingly manipulated."

I nodded. "I felt like I was becoming more lucid after I left Chesapeake City."

"That may be so," said Petrovich. "Unfortunately everyone else I've spoken with who went through something similar had a very prominent permanent effect from this medication which supposedly prevents aggression."

"How do you know so much about this?" I asked.

"We of the Friends have some contacts inside the new cities. They are few in number, but some of them have been very helpful. Many of them are scientists; some have had firsthand involvement in the development of these drugs. Others have given us some of the knowledge that we have used to keep up a food supply. This equipment," she motioned at the radio equipment that occupied much of the room, "we use it to stay in contact with them."

"I'm very impressed," I said.

"I know this is a lot for you to absorb. It must be shocking for you to learn this. We don't just fight the new order of cities because we're jealous of what they have. We fight them because of what they have done, and what they continue to do to us. You now must see this in what they've done to you. You know now that their need for order was more important in their decision calculus than your well-being."

I had to agree with this.

"Dirgo also tells me that you came to us after a fight with some peddlers of concentrate," she asked.

I nodded again.

"Concentrate is another example of the agenda of the new cities," Petrovich told me. "It does provide a modicum of nutrition, but we've found it to be addictive. What's worse, apparently the desired effect of the concentrate is to sterilize those who use it. The cities are patient; they know they have evolution on their side. So rather than actually massacring the rest of humanity, they are slowly sterilizing the population. They want to depopulate the world until their kind can retake it. The other strategic advantage of the concentrate is that ordinary citizens barter their weapons for it, allowing the new cities to prevent the possibility of a militia being mobilized against them. Their plans are well-crafted."

"There must be a cadre of leaders involved in crafting these plans."

"We don't know. Our contacts are few, and none of them are very politically active. But we can only guess that, since concentrate is being peddled in other countries, that there may be a worldwide organization to the new cities. By the same token, any move we make against any one of the new cities will resonate throughout all of them."

"Are you planning a strike against the new cities?" I asked.

"Yes we are. The time is ripe for action, and the people who follow me will soon grow tired of my words unless we can win a decisive victory soon. Dirgo can tell you more about our plans. Unfortunately, I have much more to do."

"Could I ask you one more question?"

"You can ask anything," she replied.

"Your organization... Where did you come up with the name for 'The Friends'?"

"Basically, I started the organization with a small group of other youths when I was a young woman. Most... well, all of them have since died. I used to talk about the past and mention my friends as a group. Eventually, the people who joined me felt as though, they were also like the friends I mentioned. The term as a description just developed into the namesake of the organization."

Throughout the conversation, Petrovich maintained her keen expression. I imagined she must have been carefully calculating all of my reactions to what she said. I thanked her for taking the time to talk to me, but I was still in shock over what I had learned. I had suffered so much since my excommunication from Chesapeake City. I wondered now if this suffering may have been at their hands. I supposed that, in a way, it made no difference now. I had lost all my remaining motivation to return to the new cities, and even though Belinda was still there, I had no loyalty left for Chesapeake City, much less for the other cities.

Petrovich advised me to return to the large floor that was used for dispensing food. It was nearly time for a lunch to be served, and that way, I could find my way back to Dirgo. Mainly, though, I wanted to find Troy. I wanted to share what I had just heard with someone, and I felt closer to Troy if only because of what we had shared together when we were both part of Connors' group. What Petrovich had told me filled me with an incredible feeling of relief in the knowledge that I hadn't been merely senile and ineffective as a worker in my final days in Chesapeake City.

I wanted to talk to Troy about this more than Dirgo. There was something about Dirgo that prevented me from trusting him. He had been kind to me, but I sensed that he had the potential to be manipulative. Unlike Petrovich, I thought, Dirgo must have risen in the ranks of the Friends because of his political skills. I thought of Petrovich as similar to Connors. The difference was her adherence to an ideology and her desire to lead others, not for her own glory, but to protect the rest of humanity from the new cities. Connors was much more reluctant in his role as a leader. I thought of these things as I searched around for Troy, but mostly I thought of what Petrovich had told me. I was trying to absorb and accept the truth about what happened to me. I knew somehow that what she had told me was probably the truth.

Chapter VIII

Petrovich was herself born in Rochester, New York into circumstances of horrible poverty. The fact that she was still surviving in the world was a testament to her personal strength. Petrovich's mother had immigrated to the United States with her family as a young woman. In their travel, her parents both became ill and died. Her mother was left with no family and no money as she arrived in the United States alone. After only a few months of working at the only job she could get—as a prostitute—Petrovich's mother became pregnant and couldn't even work once her pregnancy began to show. Without appropriate medical treatment, her mother delivered the baby in the presence of only another woman who was also a prostitute. Petrovich's mother died in childbirth, she was able to hold her newborn daughter for only a few minutes before she fell unconscious. The last words she uttered were, "I love you. I will always love you." There was no way that she could have predicted that her baby would survive for very long, much less that she would have the life that Petrovich found.

The newborn infant, Ida Petrovich, was brought to an orphanage by the other prostitute, Sarah Harper. As a young girl, she had a disciplined personality. She never seemed to cry or complain, and she worked hard and diligently at any chores that she was assigned to. Sarah Harper would often visit her as Petrovich grew to become a young girl. Sarah would often encourage Petrovich to behave and to be disciplined, and she constantly reminded Petrovich to be wary of following her peers when they misbehaved. Sarah, in turn, promised to try to visit more often if Petrovich behaved well. The two became increasingly close as Petrovich grew. Eventually, Harper told her the circumstances of her birth, Petrovich felt, at a very young age that she needed to do something worthwhile with her life, to justify the sacrifice that her mother made so that she could be brought into the world. The way Petrovich saw the events of her birth, her mother had given her life to give life to Petrovich.

Sarah saw her role in Petrovich's life as an educator for the young girl. Whenever she could, she visited Petrovich to discuss current events and news. Since she was also a victim of unfortunate circumstances, she thought that Petrovich should have every possible advantage. Her efforts to tell Petrovich about what was going on in the world were, in part, her attempt at giving Petrovich an education. Since she had no education in any other area, this was all she could do for the young girl. Moreover, Sarah sensed a keen brightness in the young girl that she knew would make her above average in her life. Petrovich took her visits with Sarah as something more. She felt that this woman was telling her all the things that were wrong with the world in the hopes that she might someday change them. In her youthful naiveté, Petrovich thought that, if she could correct the inequities of the world, then she could make her mother proud and justify her life. "She's always watching you," Sarah would say. "Make sure you be a good girl and make your mother proud."

In another way, Sarah was careful not to assume the role of Petrovich's mother. She knew that she couldn't be an example to the young girl, and she had difficulty avoiding the girl's questions when she would ask Sarah what she did for a living. Also, she wanted Petrovich to feel that she was loved and cared for, but she neither had the time nor the resources to give Petrovich a good upbringing. All she could do for the girl was to be a good example to her for the brief time during which the two of them interacted. Sarah always felt a void in her life since she had no children, and her body was so ravaged by a number of sexually transmitted diseases, that she could not herself carry a child. Watching Petrovich grow gave Sarah some of the rewards of motherhood without committing her to provide what she could never give to a growing child. Meanwhile Sarah had been saving some of her money, and putting it aside for Petrovich. Since she had no family, she felt she had no other purpose for any money she could save.

As Petrovich grew older, she worked hard in school. She developed a stern and disciplined personality, which was necessary for her to remain uninvolved in drugs and crime. When Petrovich was eleven, the northeast states of America and Canada were decimated by St. Lawrence fever, a viral epidemic that was spread by mosquitoes. The disease started with a disproportionately large, edematous welt from a mosquito bite. Within a few days, the victim would begin experiencing bloody vomiting and encephalitis. Within less than a week, the victim's entire body would be virtually liquefied by the disease. While insects had been an annoyance previous to that epidemic, after it, they became a deadly force. The entire population of the North American continent began to wear thick, protective clothing and even headgear. For most, however the protection was too little too late. Petrovich was one of the lucky ones. Sarah was not. As soon as Sarah realized what was happening, she emptied her savings and gave all her money to Petrovich.

Petrovich was horrified when she saw Sarah's arm, "Oh, my God!" she cried. "No. No."

Sarah gently held the young girl. "I know. I'll only have a few days left. I don't want you to cry, I want you to be strong."

Petrovich looked into Sarah's eyes, and she was calmed by the strength she saw there. Even Sarah was surprised by how much strength she herself was showing, a strength she didn't know she had in her. Sarah had always been able to act like a strong woman when she was with Petrovich, she felt the little girl needed to see someone strong to know that survival was possible in the world. But now, Sarah felt that she actually did possess a deep inner strength.

"Listen, Ida," Sarah said gently. "I want you to be strong. I've been saving some money for you; it's not enough for you to live on for very long, but I want you to use it to keep yourself safe, and to build yourself some kind of a future."

Petrovich was touched by this gesture, but still overwhelmed by grief. Finally, at Sarah's convincing, Petrovich began to calm down, and she thought of the future.

Petrovich watched and waited with Sarah as the final moments of her life elapsed. She held her hand while Sarah vomited out much of her blood. Petrovich cleaned her face off as she choked and drifted in and out of shock. Sarah was strong for most of the ordeal, but as the final moments came, she broke down and sobbed in pain and delirium. In a way, watching Sarah die such a horrible death made Petrovich even stronger. She felt a horrible injustice that a woman who had cared for her so much and been so kind would see such an abrupt painful ending to her life, and she wondered if her mother died the same way.

Sarah Harper's body was left in her small apartment for days after she died. Petrovich tried in vain to contact authorities to remove and bury her body, but at the height of the epidemic, there were too many bodies for the authorities to take care of. Moreover, few people were willing to spend the time outside that would need to be devoted to burials; most people were living in fear of the spreading disease. Other than a couple of visits to Sarah Harper's apartment, Petrovich stayed mostly indoors in her orphanage.

Months after the epidemic's peak, it still claimed victims. A vaccine was developed but, in some, the vaccine created a version of the same disease. Finally, the orphanage could no longer get food to feed its children. The orphanage was closed shortly thereafter, and the remaining, surviving children were sent to a larger facility in Annapolis. This new building was basically an old gymnasium, which was equipped with some matting for the new children to sleep on. The building itself was hardly airtight, so a number of insects and mosquitoes were able to make their way in easily. Petrovich and the other children had to wear their protective gear indoors as well as outdoors and at all times.

At the new institution, Petrovich encountered a much greater diversity of other youths. She began to find that even some of the older children had the same beliefs as her regarding politics, and she found more and more of an audience whenever she articulated her feelings. Her friends were originally a close cadre of some of the teens who were easily influenced, but loyal, and a few others who were free-thinking and shared Petrovich's thoughts.

As infrastructure decayed even further, there were only meager funds allotted to the orphanage, scarcely enough for all of the children to live on. Petrovich and the other teens finally decided it would be easier to survive outside their orphanage institution. Once in Annapolis, Petrovich and her friends began to live in an abandoned building in downtown. Petrovich used the money that Sarah Harper gave her to begin to purchase a small armamentarium of weapons, at first, for self-defense. And Petrovich became more than an ideological leader, she was developing into a formidable fighter in her own right. That was the beginning of her movement.

The Friends had developed into a very impressive organization. After my conversation with Petrovich, I was hungry as I stood in line waiting with the hundreds of others for food. My body was still replenishing itself from my weeks of malnutrition. After I ate a couple of mouthfuls, I weaved through the crowds until I found Troy. He was sitting with a group of men his age, much younger than myself. They were joking with each other infrequently, but mostly, they all looked very stern for their age. Troy shared their look. I was glad, though, when he smiled upon seeing me. He moved over to make room for me to sit down.

"Hey. Troy, I just spent some time with Petrovich."

"Really?" He seemed impressed. "What's she like? In person, I mean?" he asked.

"She's a bright, bright woman."

"Yeah," he agreed, "we're lucky to have her as a leader. What did she talk to you about?"

"Well, I wanted to tell you, but maybe I should just tell you later." I was speaking quietly and as I said this, I looked around at the young men sitting with Troy. I didn't want to blurt out the shocking revelations I had just had in front of complete strangers, nor did I want to reveal that I was once a member of the new cities.

"It's okay you can tell me." Troy responded.

"You're among Friends," said another young man at the table, smiling at me, as he said this.

"Petrovich told me that I might have been drugged while I was in Chesapeake City. Apparently, they might have given me a drug to prevent violence. But apparently, it subdued me so much that it depressed my intellect. That's what Petrovich told me."

"My god... That's shocking... But I can't say I'm too surprised. I had heard about similar things that the cities were doing. If they had their way we'd all be living under their tight order." As Troy said this, some of the other men in the group heard it and offered their agreement.

"Or they'd just take the easy route and kill the rest of us off," said another young man in the group. By this point, they had all momentarily left their food alone to hear what we were saying. I saw the look in their eyes, and for the first time, I realized the size and the gravity of the threat to the new cities that the Friends posed.

"Don't worry," said Troy to me softly. "We're all on the same side here. Just because you used to live in one of the cities, we don't hold that against you."

"I've talked to a few of the leaders of the Friends to try to give them some strategic information on the protection and defenses of the new cities," I said to Troy.

"I remember what you went through," Troy said.

I remembered how he and Patricia had seen me through several weeks of sickness after I left Chesapeake City.

"Troy," I said. "If you're going to be in on any attack that's being planned, please be careful."

Troy looked at me for a moment. "Thanks... We can't keep surviving like this. I know my best bet is to take a stand now against the cities. They're smart. They're watching us die slowly, not killing the rest of humanity at once. They think that we won't notice if they just let us die a few at a time. Are you going to help if we attack one of the new cities soon?"

"Delaware City?" I asked. This was the most likely target due to its proximity to Annapolis.

"Yes," Troy said.

"I'll try," I said.

"Maybe you shouldn't. You're a lot older than we are." Troy didn't know my actual age, which must have been even more than he was surmising. I must have looked especially weak sitting next to him. I was still malnourished and recovering from all the beatings I had undergone in Newark.

154

"Yeah, but like you said," I reminded him. "We're all in the same boat."

The other young men in the group were finishing their food by this point. Apparently, Troy and the rest of them were working on a small army of vehicles at the time. The vehicles were a heterogeneous group of cars and trucks that were the property of the Friends and were being suited with large propeller-like fans. Troy and the other young men were installing them and working on the rest of the vehicles. That's where I joined the group of them for the rest of the day. I tried to lend a hand here and there when I could be useful. I was hungrier by the end of the day, but at least I felt as though I was contributing something to the Friends. After all, I was staying with them for free and eating their food; the tactical information I had given them about the defenses of the city was probably of little help. I was very comfortable during my time with the Friends and, in many ways, I wished that it would have lasted longer.

Chapter IX

That night, I went to sleep easily as I had on all of the other nights I spent with the Friends. I was sleeping indoors; I was in a bed; and I had some amount of food in my stomach. As on any other night, I received at least a couple of new welts from whatever insects had penetrated the inside of this decaying building, but it always felt comfortable to lay down in the quarters that the Friends provided for me. As I went to sleep, I thought briefly of everything that had happened to me. I had accepted that what Petrovich had told me was true, but I was still uneasily mulling over all of it in my head. At the same moment I was both relieved and dumbfounded by the recent revelations. The world that I lived in was so different from what I perceived. I wondered what else had had been done to me while I was in Chesapeake City.

My thoughts turned to Corrina. I remembered her skin, her eyes, her mannerisms. I felt a little guilty as I realized how much better off I was than her at this moment. And, after all, it had been she who took me to the Friends in the first place. I should have found a way to express my gratitude. Thoughts of Corrina led me to sleep.

I don't remember what time it was, but I thought I must have been sleeping deeply when Dirgo awoke me. "Come with me. I have to show you something," he said. Through my drowsy, clouded thoughts, I got out of bed and followed him to an empty part of the stairwell that connected the floors of the building. I was too drowsy to take note of the thick smell of alcohol already on his breath.

Once we got to the stairwell, Dirgo produced a large metal flask from a small closet under the stairs. "Want a drink?"

I was never much of a drinker. First, alcohol has never had much of an effect on me. Second, alcohol was contraband in the new cities, and it was too expensive in the old cities for anyone to have it. Apparently, Dirgo had somehow procured a bottle though, and he beaconed me to join him for a drink. Since he and the Friends had been so good to me, I accepted a few drinks. I sipped the alcohol as it bitterly ran down my throat. Dirgo laughed at the faces I made as we talked.

Several drinks later, I asked Dirgo to explain to me what Petrovich's plans were to attack one of the new cities. He seemed surprisingly willing to divulge all of the details of her plan. "First," he said, "Petrovich is going to send a troop of men with oxygen tanks to disable the periphery. Then, a bunch of vehicles with these fans built onto them into the cloud of pesticides around Delaware City. We're going to have them drive like a big 'V' to make a trail that we can walk through. Once they get to the city wall, they'll use a bunch of guns and explosives to open up the city."

"Huh," I said.

"Whoever is in the vehicles is going to be wearing masks with oxygen tanks. Then the rest of us are supposed to charge in after them like a big army, whoever survives is supposed to storm into Delaware City." Dirgo paused for a moment. "Likely plan, eh?"

Dirgo didn't seem very enthusiastic about the plan, which seemed strange to me since he was one of the leaders of the Friends. He seemed very drunk, though. I judged that he had been drinking for a while before he woke me up. "Petrovich has a devoted little army here," I said. We might be surprised by what they could accomplish."

"They're not devoted. They're only acting loyal because the Friends give them food," Dirgo retorted. "Food that we all gobble up from insect-infested vats."

"Do you think that this offense that she's planning will fail?"

"No," he responded, at first, then more thoughtfully, he added, "I don't know. I can't predict the future. But this isn't any way for people to live—out here, outside of the new cities. They're pretty advanced—better technology, and probably better weapons than anything we have."

Throughout my time with the Friends, I sensed Dirgo's envy of those who lived in the new cities. I was now beginning to sense also Dirgo's lack of respect for the rest of the world. Before too long, the alcohol had started getting to me. I told Dirgo I was sleepy, and that I had worked hard that day; then, I went back to bed.

Dirgo was well supported during his youth. He grew up as the son of an engineer in Washington, D.C. His father's plans were focused on securing a place for himself in the new cities. His father, Simon Dirgo was a reasonably skilled engineer, but he was relying more on his savvy and personal skills to secure a place for himself in one of the new cities. Like his son, Simon Dirgo was adept at dealing with others, and he seemed to have an innate ability to blend into social circles. This was all occurring at a time when the upper middle class outside of the new cities was beginning to vanish. As society evolved, there just wasn't as much room for a middle class. Those who remained either secured a place in the new cities or perished. Simon Dirgo wasn't as acutely aware that his role in the world was vanishing, but he did know that his level of material comfort would be much higher if he were able to live in one of the new cities.

Dirgo's mother, Cecilia found most of her adult life to be a disappointment. She married Simon with the hopes of being prosperous and being able to live a comfortable life as a housewife in a social order that was becoming an anachronism. While the two were seeing each other, Cecilia let herself become pregnant. Things were going well with their relationship, and getting pregnant gave Cecilia the slight bit of leverage that she needed to make Simon commit to marriage. She was from a more poor circumstance than he was, though she was never destitute. She hoped to at least improve her material wealth and comfort by marrying Simon. Unfortunately, she found the world to be increasingly uncomfortable for her, even with the advantages that Dirgo could provide for her. Over time, she began to realize that only those citizens of the new cities had a life that was at all comfortable, by her standards. It didn't take long for her perspective on the new cities to evolve into envy, and she saw her marriage as a failed investment.

One could only apply to live in one of the new cities every few years, depending on the city, and the application process was always very difficult. Usually, after three rejections, you couldn't reapply to be a resident in one of the new cities. Simon had applied as frequently as he could, but he had already received two rejections, and a third one would have resigned him to his fate outside of the new cities forever. He would have no place in the lifeboats of humanity and would be left to sink with the remainder of the masses.

Fueled on by a few uncommon stories of those who were accepted into one of the new cities after two rejections, Simon was still hopeful. But by the time their son Jon was ten, the Dirgo family received its third rejection. Simon Dirgo was devastated. Cecilia acted supportive for a few months, but even if her emotional support had been sincere, it would not have been enough for Simon to be encouraged after this rejection. Simon turned to drinking, which he always had a propensity to do, but he now spent more time, and much more money on his alcoholism. Cecilia continued to support Simon and, oddly, throughout this period she seemed unconcerned.

As it turned out, unbeknownst to her husband, Cecilia had met someone else, an older, much more gifted engineer, who was applying to live in the new cities for the first time after developing several very promising patents. Cecilia knew he would have a better chance of securing a position in the new cities, and she was attracted to his successfulness. A few months after he was informed of his acceptance, Cecilia left her husband with no notice. All that he had left of her was a note that told him she needed to be with someone who would be a better provider.

Simon plunged even further into drinking after his wife left him. So much so that his relationship with his son began to suffer. Throughout Jonathan's upbringing, Simon Dirgo loved him very much; he looked at his son as having the potential to do great things—the same way he thought about himself when he was younger.

Simon also began to resent his son as a reason he was rejected by the new cities. It was possible that having a son hurt the Dirgo's chances of getting into one of the new cities. Children, after all, can't contribute or be productive. So when a city accepts a family with children, they have to also accept residents who won't be able to contribute to the workforce for some time. In reality, Simon's fatherhood made little difference in the decision calculus of the cities. Simon Dirgo magnified it in his own mind, though and blamed his son for the lost opportunity to live in the new cities and for the loss of his wife. Now it would be almost impossible for Simon to even reapply to live in the cities, and he became increasingly despondent and unaffectionate towards Dirgo.

In the meantime, Jonathan Dirgo's life underwent many changes, which he could only partially understand. His mother was gone, and his father was drunk and angry with him. What little material comfort that he once had with his family would soon be lost by his father's drinking habit and growing apathy. At least Jon had inherited his father's political savvy and skills in dealing with others, and he was growing up to be a bright young man in his own right. His father also instilled his own value system in his son. Simon prioritized material comfort and raised his son to admire and envy the wealthier classes in the new cities. Jonathan adopted this value system easily as his own.

Dirgo's father died when Jonathan was fifteen. He had squandered most of his savings by drinking and he had all but lost his job before he died. He was outside of his home for a walk after a bout of drinking, when he collapsed and fell unconscious. The few possessions he had were stolen, and his body was attacked by insects. He regained consciousness a few times to experience the pain of the insects tearing tiny bites out of his flesh. He could feel them piecing apart his body through his drunken haze. He might have survived this incident, but he had little will to live left, and so he let himself lapse into death. As his life flashed before his eyes, he realized how much he had failed in achieving the goals he set for himself and his hopes of attaining wealth. His death now underscored the tragic shortcomings of his life.

Unfortunately, Simon Dirgo also left little money for his son to live on after he passed away. The money he left was scarcely enough for Jonathan to pay the rent in his family's home for even one more month. Soon, Dirgo was evicted. He had nowhere to go and insufficient training to get a job. He spent some time languishing in the streets. It was only through blind luck that Dirgo was taken in by the Friends.

On one particularly bad night, Dirgo was beat up and mugged by some thieves, and left unconscious to suffer the same death that his father endured only a few months earlier. Fortunately, his body was found by some of the Friends, who fed him and cleaned his wounds. Though the Friends cared very closely for him, Dirgo never completely regained his health. He was grateful, though. With the Friends, Dirgo had a marginally better level of material wealth.

Once he was a member of the Friends, Dirgo easily rose up in their ranks by doing what he knew he did best. He got along well with others, and he was naturally articulate. Soon, more and more members found him to be a good source of leadership. Even Petrovich was impressed with his oratorical skills and persuasiveness as he espoused her ideology. Once Dirgo had a foothold in the Friends, he had a way of restoring a modicum of material comfort in his life, and Dirgo was grateful for what the Friends were giving him. Although it wasn't the material comfort of his youth, or the abundance that he envied in the new cities, it was something.

For me, the next few weeks of my life with the Friends gave me a pattern to follow, and gave my days a routine. I would work with the Friends equipping and repairing their vehicles. I ate, sometimes twice a day; and I had a good place to sleep. This was, arguably, the most comfortable I had been since leaving Chesapeake City. Troy's friends and I became closer the more we worked together. I talked more with Dirgo while I was with the Friends. He was a little less tolerable when he was drunk, but there was a kinship between us, I guess because we were both older than almost everyone else was and also because we had a mutual respect for Petrovich. I wondered how Dirgo had risen to such a high rank in the Friends. He seemed aggressive and ambitious, unlike Petrovich, who by comparison was totally selfless in her devotion to her cause.

I even had a few more conversations with Petrovich. She was meticulous in her planning, considering everything from the direction of the wind currents to the chemical composition of the pesticide cloud that surrounded Delaware City. She knew an amazing amount of information about the people whom she was sending into battle, partially because she was entrusting them with a great responsibility, but possibly also because she knew she was sending many of them to their death. I was always impressed with her insight into people and he visions of the future of humanity, but she was equally able to consider science, physics, and chemistry, in conceiving her plans. My growing friendship with Petrovich was another reason why I enjoyed being with the Friends so much.

Petrovich would soon want to make good on her promise to lead an offensive against one of the new cities, but none of us were given notice of when this attack would occur. Finally, on one morning Petrovich woke up and told one of her assistants that she would launch the offensive the next day. No large-scale announcement was made, or needed to be. The news spread among the Friends within minutes.

The preparation for the attack had been on going for some time. One group of young men, some of the healthier members of the Friends had been trained for quite some time to be the drivers of the vehicles that comprised the front line of Petrovich's assault. The next line was going to be another group of able-bodied men, who were going to be equipped with gas masks and oxygen tanks to provide some protection against the chemical wall that stood protecting the elite within the new cities. This group of men was going to be carrying bomb launchers to destroy the turbines and pesticide pumps that maintained the chemical cloud. Behind them would be the rest of the army carrying whatever weapons and tools, they could hold. Petrovich was planning the first few lines to cut into the chemical cloud like a "V". Oxygen and gas masks were limited, so only the front lines would be well protected. The rest of the army would try to pierce through whatever corridor of relatively clean air the front lines could open up. The same day, people were being transported into Annapolis by the truckload from a handful of other nearby cities, including Newark. Hundreds of new faces arrived, and as I saw them pass me by, I wondered if Corrina would be one of them.

The atmosphere among the Friends changed quickly. Everyone around me was overcome by a frenzied, aggressive kind of energy. I watched while Troy's friends talked angrily about the way they would make the people of New Delaware pay for discarding the rest of humanity. I felt at times, like I was lost among strangers when I heard people talking like this, but I knew the reasons for their feelings.

Petrovich was preparing herself for the coming conflict as well. She and some of her close advisers were going to be in the rear of the offensive. Petrovich actually wanted to be in the midst of her people, helping to lead in the attack, but finally she succumbed to pressure from her advisers to stay back behind the battle. Although her mind was strong, she was physically weak and frail from her long life of adversity. She, Dirgo, and I were going to be in a jeep immediately behind her army.

In my more doubtful moments I realized that the odds were heavily stacked against Petrovich. On the other hand, I knew that the rest of the Friends felt like Troy and the other young men. They were going to die eventually anyway, and if they lived a long life, it would be a long, uncomfortable life. That's what made the Friends such a dangerous weapon: they had so little to lose.

Many of us stayed up late the night before the offensive. It was difficult to sleep with the anticipation of the task ahead of us. I bumped into Troy as I was roaming around that night. His life seemed precious in my eyes, since he survived when the rest of Connors group was killed. Looking at him, I saw parts of Connors, Patricia, and the others living on in a small way.

"Hey, Troy," I said to him.

"Hi," he answered somberly.

"Are you worried about tomorrow?" I asked.

"Sort of." He answered hesitantly, "I guess I shouldn't be."

"Well, it's natural to be nervous." I didn't want to say what I was thinking, that Troy might not survive through the next day.

"Yeah," he answered. "But the way I look at it, we'll just do what we can."

"You'll be fighting a good fight." I looked at Troy and saw an aged, pensive man, not the strong, young energetic boy I had known just a short time ago. Some of the other young men were letting the adrenaline take control more than Troy; he was somber and reflective.

Troy looked at me and smiled as I said this.

"Listen, Troy," I continued, "be careful." Troy was going to be one of the men on foot carrying weapons. I wanted to offer him a safer position with myself in the rear of the battle lines. "We need people to be with Petrovich and the rest of the leaders, if you want…"

"Thanks," he said, cutting me off. "I'm sure I'll be alright." He knew he was only giving me false reassurance. He couldn't predict the outcome of the battle, and moreover, neither one of us could have expected the turn of events that would follow.

I wished Troy good luck for the next day. It seemed like a weak gesture, but I couldn't think of anything else to say. I was worried I might not see him again.

Although I was sleeping deeply every night while I stayed with the Friends, I seldom remembered my dreams. That night I had difficulty falling asleep, but once I did, I had a dream that I remembered clearly afterwards. I was inside one of the new cities, but it was greener and less sterile than I remembered Chesapeake City being. There were gardens and lush vegetation, and I felt a sense of peace. No one from the new cities was around. Instead, I was surrounded by Petrovich, Troy, Connors, some young men from the Friends, and the rest of Connors' group. I guess that, in the dream, I imagined I was in Delaware City. I saw Petrovich as a beautiful, young woman. Patricia and Troy were holding hands and laughing together, and Connors was watching with the look of a proud father in his eyes.

I woke up deeply saddened by the reality that I was facing. I tried to convince myself that this was a prediction of what would come to pass in the future. I knew Connors and his group were gone forever, but I thought that my dream could be a vision of Petrovich's victory, and the world she could establish with the Friends with the technology of the new cities. Much as I tried to convince myself to the contrary, I had seen a great deal of death since leaving Chesapeake City, and I couldn't shake the fear that I would see more the next day.

Chapter X

The next morning, the atmosphere of frenzied anger changed to quiet anxiety. An uncomfortable silence permeated the community.

Over the previous night, hundreds more people had arrived, maybe even thousands. There was scarcely room on the floor for the newcomers to sleep, and many of them probably didn't sleep at all. One of the floors of the building we were in was a makeshift mess hall where the food was usually given out. We never had breakfast, but now we were all facing a long day. Of course, there was seldom enough food for everyone, even less so with so many more people. I didn't opt to eat, since I knew I was going to be on one of the back lines of people who were going to stay close to Petrovich. Most of the people who were going to be closer to the front lines would probably need their energy more than I. I headed upstairs to the floor from which Petrovich was going to speak to begin the day. She was waiting on the balcony with her speakers and microphones already set up. Her thin frame was leaning over the side of the balcony railing looking down at the relatively quiet streets below. Some of her other followers were beginning to congregate around her and on the streets below. Dirgo had not yet arrived.

She turned to me, "You've lived in the cities; you penetrated the perimeter of a city. Tell me, the truth. The movement we've organized is a weapon. How do you think it will do against their defenses?"

"You have a lot of followers," I replied, "a lot of able-bodied men. I was thinking to myself, how little we all have left to lose. That makes us very dangerous." I was hoping also to convey that, despite my short time in her organization, I felt very much a part of her struggle.

She smiled at me in response, knowing that I wanted to provide encouragement.

"I know that you've already considered the odds realistically," I added. "You're not overestimating the chances that you have. But I think that there's a lot of loyalty here. The people here are ready to fight for you."

Petrovich's army had many advantages. Not only were they loyal and dedicated, also, they were a group of people that knew adversity well. The population of the new cities was spoiled, and unwilling to sacrifice themselves in battle; they wouldn't be able to fight like the Friends could.

"This is our last chance," she said. "If we fail to act by this point, we will soon dwindle in strength and enthusiasm. My speeches only hold so much weight for these people, and that weight is poorly inadequate compared to the weight of the walls that surround the new cities."

In the brief time I knew Petrovich, she never gave a hint of any anxiety or insecurity. Now, for the first time, I saw these emotions slowly taking hold on her face. I knew that she took her commitment to the Friends very seriously. Her movement was the last chance that a part of humanity had for survival, and it was riding on her leadership. I placed my hand on hers.

People were beginning to gather in the streets below us, anticipating the speech Petrovich was about to give. The day was going to be long as well as the journey ahead of us to Delaware City, and Petrovich wanted to waste no time in beginning it.

"Where's Dirgo?" she asked moments before she would commence her speech.

The rest of Petrovich's assistants didn't know and, apparently, no one had seen him that day.

"I may need you to begin my speech," she said to me looking somewhat worried once again. I didn't want to remind her that it might shake the people's faith if they saw me giving her introduction and not Dirgo. I was sure she had already calculated this. By this point, it seemed unlikely that Dirgo could be quickly found. For a few moments I was infuriated by the thought that Dirgo would back out of his association with the Friends. He had already told me his faith in the Friends was weak, but I couldn't have guessed how little loyalty he had. Petrovich must have sensed this concern in the others, but she didn't let it affect her. I realized that the task ahead of the Friends was too important for me to be concerned over the commitment of one man.

"I'll do whatever you need," I replied. None of the other Friends would have been able to give a speech on such little notice. Although the faith and courage of the people around me was strong, no one here was much of a speaker. The Friends were afflicted by a life of the same diseases and poverty that stole the souls of all the residents of the old cities that I had met.

Petrovich turned her attention to her assistants and confidantes on the balcony before addressing those on the street below. "Friends, before I begin this day, I want to thank you for your unwavering courage and support for me. We have all come through trying times to arrive at this day, and we have been through trying times together. Now, the depth of our convictions will be tested. More important than our strategic advantages, our preparation, and our ability to surprise the leadership of the new cities, we have a cause that is right. This cause will carry us through our battle today."

Her followers looked relieved as she said this—reminding them that she was the backbone of their movement and that her conviction was strong. I was trying, in the meantime, to think of words to say to introduce her.

"It is time for us to begin," Petrovich said to me.

I've never been much of a politician. To be honest, I've never thought of myself as charismatic. Moreover, I had never spoken to more than five or six people at a time, much less a crowd the size of Petrovich's organization. I moved out towards the podium. There were cheers from the crowd in anticipation of the address they were about to receive. I was speechless as I looked at the mass of people, their faces indistinct as they jostled into the streets. As I stood, receiving their applause, a passing mosquito landed on my neck. I didn't feel its fine legs on my skin until after it delivered its sting. I raised my hand to slap my neck. The sting brought me out of my nervous trance, and I started to speak to the crowd below.

"Friends," I started, "let us carry courage in our battle today, and let our courage be strengthened by the knowledge that we are fighting for what's right." I could hear some cheers from the audience. I turned back to look at Petrovich. "Now, let us hear from the leader who has brought us this far, and who will bring us victory today." I was surprised by the tone of my own voice as I said this and realized that I truly felt a connection to this organization.

The crowd's enthusiasm grew as I spoke, and Petrovich stepped toward the microphones.

"My Friends," spoke Petrovich, "today is truly an historic day. What we do now, whether we fail or not in our battle, will be recorded for the rest of history. History..." she paused. "It's an important force, and one that the new cities fail to see. They fail to see the common history that they have shared with the rest of humanity. They fail to see the strengths of democracy and community. They fail to see the weaknesses of clandestine elitism. And they fail to see that we are the next wave of history—a rising tide that will change their fate and the fate of humanity." Petrovich's words masterfully controlled the mood of the entire audience.

"To those who have joined us from throughout the continent, thank you. To those who have spread the messages to others about our cause, thank you. To those who have only recently joined our ranks, thank you. I do not only thank you from my own heart, I also thank you on behalf of the race that you are standing up for.

"We have two advantages as we fight today—two keys that will lead us to victory. First, our cause is right. We are fighting against elitism. We are fighting against inequality. We are fighting for the innumerable lives that have been lost needlessly to malnutrition and disease while a wealthy few who live in material excess find ways to hoard even more resources. The second key to our victory today is our will to survive. The cities have a lot to lose today—their material comfort, their wealth. We have nothing left to lose. Even our survival, our last possession, which we will fight for today is threatened. If we fail today we will lose our only, and our last chance at surviving like this or in any other state. The cities are not prepared to sacrifice anything in pursuit of victory, but we have already sacrificed everything in our lives just to hold on to our existences.

"So look around you, to your fellow Friends, those people standing on all sides of you will be remembered in history for their greatness—for the size of their character. All of our efforts have been culminating to this moment on whose brink we are now perched. To victory!" I could hear the collective cheer swelling in the audience's voices. I could hear them yelling and chanting for victory.

I looked at Petrovich in amazement through out her speech. She had risen through extremely adverse circumstances, and become an intellectual giant. I imagined all the good she could do in a world less broken than the one she lived in.

Within an hour, all of Petrovich's army was poised on the edge of Annapolis, and everyone was in the appropriate gear and position. Dirgo still hadn't arrived, but our excitement and enthusiasm now outweighed concern for finding him. I imagined that, deep down, Petrovich must have felt that he had doubts and fears about attacking Delaware City. She was a perceptive woman. I would wonder later how much she knew about Dirgo's doubts.

It took the army several hours to reach the limits of the perimeter of Delaware City. Much of this time was made in silence. The people I saw marching were looking to the horizon as they walked, as if trying to focus on a distant object. Closer to Delaware City, I could feel the chemicals collecting in my throat as I breathed in the pesticide-saturated air. This smell had a special meaning to me, as I remembered I almost lost my life the last time I sensed it. Several men began to cough and choke. Petrovich and I weren't doing as badly since we were in the back of the group. I was extremely nauseated, as I recalled my previous exposure to these same chemicals outside of Chesapeake City where I was left for dead. I resisted the urge to vomit, as a film of chemicals began collecting on my skin and clothes. We weren't to use our oxygen until it was absolutely necessary, but when the pesticides became heavier in the air, Petrovich ordered the front lines of vehicles to turn on their turbines and blow the chemical cloud away from us and toward Delaware City. The city was surrounded by a controlled field of ionizing radiation, which served to partially break down some of the chemicals in the insecticides, if they blew towards it.

Eventually, the chemical cloud engulfed us—so much so that it became more difficult to see the front lines. At this point, Petrovich finally ordered the front lines to put on their oxygen gear. Petrovich and I were in her jeep, and I could see, when I stood up, that the chemical cloud, was being somewhat divided by the turbines on the vehicles in front of us, but we weren't clearing enough air. Our next move was to get close enough to the city to launch some explosives at the turbines on the perimeter of New Delaware that were blowing the insecticides towards us.

As we edged further, we couldn't yet visualize the city, but we saw some objects through the haze in front of us. Frightened screams cut through the crowds from the front lines, and Petrovich was cut with fear with each scream, suspecting the danger ahead. We continued to advance, but it was now apparent that Delaware City was ready for our attack. An army of well-armed vehicles and armored hovercrafts was surrounding the front lines and was launching a barrage of weaponry. Through my tearing eyes, I could see the silhouettes of frightened men and women running as they emerged from the midst of the chemical cloud. The sound of the gunfire and explosions ahead was growing, as were the screams from the dying in the front lines.

"Dirgo sold us out," I heard some of Petrovich's followers say.

Petrovich was busily directing the front lines to retreat in an organized way. She had prepared her followers and herself for this scenario. We still couldn't make out what was going on ahead of us. Though there had been much training and preparation for this day, the frightened men and women on foot forgot their training and were now running away in every direction.

"We've got to get out of here," I said to Petrovich. "Listen to me, I don't think we'll survive if we stay." The sound of gunfire was louder as we continued advancing. "We've got to retreat." More silhouettes of vehicles were appearing through the chemical fog. Perhaps because of my previous near-death experience in a similar chemical fog, I was much more frightened than Petrovich. I had lost much of my will to live, but I didn't want to die like this.

"I'm staying. You can go if you want," she answered me as she dismounted from the jeep.

"You'll die here. The Friends will die with you," I was yelling at this point, the noises of the massacre ahead of us were growing closer.

"This was our movement's last chance. We won't be able to rebuild after this. I won't have another chance to bring down the cities."

"Come on you can still live and fight another day." I was now trying to pull her back onto the jeep. Some of her small army was trying unsuccessfully to retreat past the armored vehicles that were now engulfing them. They were all brutally and efficiently gunned down as they ran and as the tanks grew closer.

"I'm an old woman," she replied. "This was my last chance. I led them all here. I'll share their fate."

I looked across the crowd and realized I was beholding a massacre. Some of the vehicles were driving past us now; the field I saw around me was becoming covered with injured bodies. I was standing looking at Petrovich. A number of others were beginning to pile into the jeep that Petrovich and I had been driving. I pulled on her arm as I climbed into the driver's seat. The people in the jeep were now shouting, "Come on!" and "Let's go!"

"Leave me here," Petrovich said to me. "Please." I finally decided to honor her request. Part of my response was out of fear; the rest was in admittance of what Petrovich was saying. The tanks were now virtually surrounding us, if we didn't escape at that moment, then we would have no other chance. Petrovich turned her attention back to the Friends. She was now trying to organize the retreat and to urge her followers to retaliate with their weapons. I saw the frantic frenzy around her, though, and realized that as persuasive as she was, fear now had more control than she did over the Friends.

I tried to pick up a few more people—anyone who could hold on to the sides of the jeep. Within seconds, the inside and outside of the vehicle was covered with terrified Friends. I wanted to find Troy too, but he was probably closer to the front lines, and the odds of finding him were minimal. Certain death was just behind us.

All of the passengers in the jeep were now screaming. At least ten or so others were jumping in front of the jeep or clinging to it trying to get on board, but we couldn't save them all. I could barely maneuver and dodge my way around the rest, but we had to keep moving. I knew I wasn't saving any lives by swerving to avoid those on foot. Their deaths would most likely be delivered in a matter of moments. I was too frightened to even turn around to see the massacre behind us as the tanks and hovercrafts edged closer.

I felt now like I was in a lifeboat on a sinking ship. For an instant, I felt a painful hint of irony. I was now in a similar position as the cities, bobbing in a lifeboat while they watch the rest of their people die around them; I remembered having this same feeling while I lived in Chesapeake City. I drove out of the crowd and as far away as I could from the chemical cloud around us, back to Annapolis. Slowly, the sounds of death grew more distant.

I was horrified, but I was cheating death yet again. This time I had left Troy and Petrovich, and probably also Corrina behind. I didn't have the time or wherewithal to look and see if I knew any of the other passengers on the jeep.

I drove out of the crowds of people as we were attacked, both by Friends who knew they were being left for dead, and by the tanks that were still launching a barrage of shells. Some people on the jeep were hit by shrapnel and debris as we drove off. We made it back to Annapolis, though. Once the immediate danger had passed, I realized I didn't know any of the other passengers. I'm sure they were all grateful for their lives, but there was a strange sense among us once we realized we were out of danger. It didn't seem like anyone among us knew anyone else. A handful of others made it back. A lot of the larger trucks didn't. Thousands must have died, I thought to myself. I decided to drive us back to the building that was the Friends headquarters. When we arrived, I dropped my head down against the steering wheel of the jeep.

Some of the others in the jeep got out and started walking around. Everyone had a look of dumbfounded shock on his or her faces. I imagined that they must have been silently criticizing Petrovich for leading them into a massacre, but I knew better. Soldiers who come home after a war speak of survival guilt. The few of us who made it back to the Friends headquarters, knew that most of the people we had worked with and befriended were now dead.

It was clear that Delaware City was prepared for our attack. Coupled with my other suspicions, and his absence, I knew the reason for their preparedness was Dirgo. Just like Petrovich's followers said, he sold the movement out. Somewhere, where I couldn't see him, he was probably about to start a life of tremendous newfound material comfort. I wished I could show him the pain and death that he helped cause. I was angry and confused and I had just let a good woman—a great person—die in the pesticide smog outside of Delaware City.

"What now?" The man next to me, who was one of the first to get in the jeep, interrupted my train of thought, which was just as well. My anger and frustration wouldn't bring back the hundreds or thousands who were now lying dead. I looked over at him and saw how young he was, probably just barely in his twenties.

"I don't know," I said to him.

"You were close to Ida Petrovich, right?" he asked.

"Yeah," I said. I was wondering how he knew this.

"Are we going to be able to keep the movement going?"

"I don't know," I said. I was too tired to want to reply.

"You could still lead us. Especially if you knew Ida Petrovich well."

I didn't take the idea seriously. "No," I said, "I'm not the type to be political." I felt bad for the people around me; they had put much faith in Petrovich's leadership and vision. It should have paid off. Their faith in justice and fairness should have paid off.

Slowly, this young man—my last passenger—got out of the car. I felt bad for breaking down what must have been one of his last strands of hope.

I drove the jeep inside the main building. I knew where some extra fuel was kept and I grabbed a few gallons. It would be enough to get me somewhere else. In a few hours, maybe even a few minutes, the rest of the army of hovercraft that we had just seen would trace us back to the Friends' headquarters in

Annapolis. I grabbed a dolly and piled on a few more gallons—as much as I thought would fit. Finally, I used the rest of the gasoline that I could find to fill up the tank.

As I was pouring in the last few drops of a gallon, I heard footsteps behind me, and a familiar click. Before turning around, I felt for the weapon that I had strapped to my leg. It seemed silly now, but I remembered I had taken a small pistol with me when the Friends left for Delaware City. We all needed weapons, and I was lucky enough to end up with one. It would have been meager help in the fields outside of Delaware City if I had thought to use it sooner.

Quickly, I pulled out my gun and, with it drawn, I turned around to see that some homeless person had come in behind me. He did not seem to be a member of the Friends. More likely, he was probably here to pillage what he could—somehow knowing that most, if not all of the organization was away from the building at this point. I knew already that the click was produce from him charging up a weapon of his own. It was a small steel box with an opening in its front; similar to the one I had been attacked with when I first arrived in Newark.

Since I surprised him, his hand wasn't in a position to trigger the weapon. I was looking at him down the barrel of my small pistol, and I knew I could fire off a shot before his next move. Standing there, threatening his life, I remembered watching Jonas kill a poor, old, homeless man as he threw him off of the top of a building. I also remembered how I beat up an old woman for a morsel of food.

"Don't shoot," he said. I could see that he had performed some decision calculus in his head and had arrived at the same conclusion as I—that I could easily fatally would him before he responded.

"Drop it, then," I said.

He didn't do what I told him. Thinking back now, I don't remember if he was hesitating, or if he was moving to fire his weapon. I couldn't tell either way. As soon as he flicked his hand, I fired off a shot aiming for his little steel box. My shot halfway hit his hand and halfway hit the top of the machine, which was strapped to his shoulder. It fell to the floor and he scurried away like a frightened cockroach, without bothering to look back at me.

I felt bad for what I did. I didn't want to shoot him. I had seen enough violence in my life, and more than a lifetime's worth on that day. I wasn't that good a shot; it was only luck that made the bullet hit the top of his weapon, rather than his torso. As I stood there for a moment, I realized I was letting go of whatever contrived notion of morality I once had. Now, I was a killer, just like Jonas, just like Dirgo, just like the drivers of the countless tanks that had just massacred Petrovich's organization. These thoughts only lasted moments though, for the sake of my own survival, I had to return to the task at hand.

After the homeless man scurried off, and I finished filling the tank, I walked over to his weapon, which was now on the floor—harmless now without someone to activate it. I thought it would be valuable to keep, so I picked it up and placed it in the jeep, being careful not to touch the blood of its last owner, a few drops of which were now drying in a speckled pattern on the top of the instrument.

I decided to leave instead of stalling any further. Whoever was left in the Friends would have to fend for themselves, I thought. I drove the jeep back around to the side of the building to pick up the young man who I was talking to earlier.

"Come here," I beckoned when I found him not too far from where he exited the jeep. He approached. "Listen," I told him, "those tanks are going to be following us here after they finish off the rest of the Friends. If you want I'll take you somewhere else and drop you off."

"You're leaving?" he asked.

"Yes. We won't survive a second battle with them."

"No," he said, and then hesitated for a moment as if lost in thought. "I'll stay." He looked at me with a look that was both sad and curious at the same time.

"Look there's not going to be another chance. When they come back, they might just kill everyone in the area. You can hide somewhere here, but you'd be better off going somewhere else. I can take you somewhere."

He refused again. I didn't want to leave anyone behind, but my further requests only seemed to make him look more deeply saddened. I made a similar announcement and offer to some other people who were standing around, but they didn't want to leave either. I didn't really understand this. It seemed silly to me to escape such a horrible massacre so narrowly only to be killed a few minutes later, but no one listened. They had probably seen enough violence and decay. By suggesting survival, I was only offering to them a way to prolong their suffering. Like the young man, they probably had no more will to live, anyway. I wondered briefly how and why I still had a will to live, weak as it was.

Within a few minutes, I was back on the road, but now I was driving away from Annapolis in the opposite direction of Delaware City.

As I would have predicted, The Friends didn't last after that day. A few people vied for leadership, but none had the charisma or the intelligence to put together any kind of movement in Annapolis or elsewhere. For a few months, groups of up to five or six people would gather in Annapolis and other cities to plan to reorganize, but most of these groups didn't last long. The road ahead seemed long for the organization, and the cause of saving humanity, much less oneself, was hardly worth the effort now.

Petrovich had a gift in her ability to move people to action. She also had knowledge of the sciences, which allowed her to hydroponically engineer food. Much as I now hated to agree with Dirgo, it was the ability of the Friends to provide food for their followers that helped the organization stay cohesive. Even though the food was infested with insects, it was nourishment. That was really the bottom line. Some other movements started up briefly; the poor would continue to make pleas to the new affluent elite, but as I observed in the Delaware City incident, weaponry would always be the answer to the pleas of the impoverished.

Petrovich was right in a way. The Friends were the last chance that humanity had for equitable distribution of resources. She was wrong, though, about the historical importance of her movement.

History never remembered the Friends or Petrovich. But the stage of history had little space left for humanity, much less the pathetic final moments of our existence, which we ended up spending on our quibbling for food. The only legacy that Petrovich, a great woman, left behind was a handful of confused, lost individuals who once called themselves Friends.

Dirgo spent many more years of his life living happily with material comforts he had never before known. He had some trouble making friends in the new cities. Most of the affluent found him crude and uncivilized. Otherwise, he did well for himself for the rest of his life. The fate I wished on him wouldn't have been so rosy. I was hoping that he would be involved in some sort of violent crime once he was in the new cities. That way, he would have been drugged the same way I was, and I could have known that the cycle of my life was repeating itself, in a way, in someone else's life. On the other hand, I probably shouldn't have wished my life on any one else. After all, I didn't want my own life even for myself.

Although the Friends languished, the new cities didn't have much time left on the stage of human history either. They didn't realize it, at the time, but their role was all but played out before too long. No one should have been surprised as the insects won the race for survival against human technology. While humans could adapt, our species could no longer evolve; the insects could still do both. Over time, hoards of insects began appearing which were far less sensitive to the flimsy walls of pesticides that the cities erected or the walls of electricity and radiation that the cities were equally proud of. Some of these insects were more dangerous and more threatening than any of their fellow species had ever been. Once insects pierced the cities' defenses en masse, humanity had lost its last foothold.

All the agricultural technology of the new cities became outmoded as well. Over time, crops were overtaken by tenacious weeds, which were toxic if ingested. These new generations of plant life seized the same genetic advantages that humans had engineered into their own crops. As food in the new cities became scarce, members of the elite were more subdivided into groups of ultra-elite that could still afford sufficient food. The divisiveness in the new cities eventually led to their downfall. The few remaining humans living outside of the new cities watched this decline with little sympathy.

Needless to say, the rest of civilization living in the old cities and the wilderness in between the old cities suffered the same way. Concentrate was a good idea; after a few generations, the population was decimated. The poor had always been reproducing faster than the rich had; concentrate reversed their population expansion. In a way, the cities' plans backfired. After all, the key to survival as the world changed would have been more evolution and adaptation. With a smaller population, humanity had even less of a chance to adapt and evolve. Ironically, the new cities were only speeding up the demise that nature had planned for humanity.

Even if it hadn't been for the plans of the new cities, the rest of humanity didn't have much of a potential for a future. The increasing onslaught of insects was even more profoundly felt among the general population. Some people were so horribly disfigured by their daily exposure to insect stings that they looked to be gargoyles or demons rather than humans. More and more, people started killing each other for food.

I know there are a lot of untidy endings, though. Perhaps Troy survived. The odds were slim, but he had, after all, survived against similar odds when the rest of Connors' band was killed. For that matter, perhaps Patricia survived, although this was an even less likely scenario. Perhaps, even Petrovich survived. No one left had any vested interest in marking their deaths with the memorial that they deserved or even with a grave. They died as silently as if they had died in the wilderness with no one else around. Jonas died with the rest of humanity. His chances of survival remained only slightly better than those around him, until the odds no longer played out in his favor.

Although I had weapons and a vehicle, my life was now, more than ever, without a purpose. The only people I had ever admired, like Connors or Petrovich, had a sort of silent knowledge that they were speeding towards their own death. In a sense, Petrovich knew she was going to die there outside of Delaware City. In another sense, Connors probably also foresaw his death in the plans he had of going to the northwest. Unfortunately, this story isn't about survival; it's about suicide—the ways that everyone, including the human population, sped towards death, either by killing themselves or by killing other humans. I finally realized that day, as I drove out of Annapolis, that the will to survive was futile—that survival meant only forestalling one's inevitable death and prolonging a life of suffering.

As I said, I drove the jeep I had as far away from Annapolis as I could before my story ended in a similar way. I pulled up the covering on the jeep and slept for a few hours before I decided what to do. Having a jeep and sufficient fuel with me, I decided my only option left was to travel to the northwest part of the continent. I remembered how Patricia used to tell me that there was territory out there that was less saturated with a human population. I hoped to find some other settlements of humanity, or at least live off of the land. I didn't get very far in this last part of my quest.

Within a few days, I met my death on an isolated strip of highway. I had been sleeping during the daylight, which was probably a mistake, when a band of thugs on a truck came across me. I had fought before in my life, sometimes well, sometimes unsuccessfully. When they came upon me, I saw no reason to make the effort to fight. Their faces as they neared me looked familiar, indistinguishable from the countless disheveled figures I had seen throughout the old cities.

As they ran up to me, they wasted little time in beating my head, torso, and limbs after I stopped moving—playing possum. They hesitated for a moment. That was long enough for me to produce my pistol. Before they could get far enough away, I fired a round into my fuel, igniting it and taking my assailants to hell with me in the fireball that quickly engulfed all of us.

My final thoughts were a vague hope that these were the same thugs that wiped out Connors' band on another highway. I hoped that, if they were, then some vague justice would be served by their deaths. I didn't mind now taking my own life. I wondered even how much my attackers minded having their lives taken. I imagined that they wouldn't mind much. I had as strong a will to live as anyone I had met, but even my survival instinct was now taxed beyond its limits.

In a very small way, I was proud that I was facing a similar death that Connors faced a few months earlier. My remains were left on the side of a highway in the wilderness, without a grave, and without a memorial.

About the Author

Jabi Elijah Shriki was born in Rabat, Morocco. As a child he moved with his family to Toronto, Canada, where he was raised until the age of fifteen, when he came to the United States. From the age of seventeen to twenty-two, Jabi traveled across America and resided in over fifteen different cities.

At the age of twenty-two he began medical school at the University of Texas, and graduated at the age of twenty-six. Currently, Dr. Shriki resides in Southern California, where he works as a radiology resident.

He may be emailed at <jabi_elijah@yahoo.com>.